CROSSING
THE WIRE

BOOKS BY WILL HOBBS

Changes in Latitudes
Bearstone
Downriver
The Big Wander
Beardance
Kokopelli's Flute
Far North
Ghost Canoe
Beardream
River Thunder
Howling Hill
The Maze
Jason's Gold
Down the Yukon
Wild Man Island
Jackie's Wild Seattle
Leaving Protection

CROSSING THE WIRE

Will Hobbs

📚 HarperCollins*Publishers*

Library of Congress Cataloging-in-Publication Data

Hobbs, Will.

Crossing the wire / by Will Hobbs.— 1st ed.

p.   cm.

Summary: Fifteen-year-old Victor Flores journeys north in a desperate attempt to cross the Arizona border and find work in the United States to support his family in central Mexico.

ISBN-10: 0-06-074138-4 (trade bdg.) — ISBN-13: 978-0-06-074138-9 (trade bdg.)

ISBN-10: 0-06-074139-2 (lib. bdg.) — ISBN-13: 978-0-06-074139-6 (lib. bdg.)

[1. Voyages and travels—Fiction. 2. Survival—Fiction. 3. Illegal aliens—Fiction. 4. Mexicans—Fiction. 5. Best friends—Fiction. 6. Friendship—Fiction.] I. Title.

PZ7.H6524Cro 2006   2005019697

[Fic]—dc22   CIP

                                                                                        AC

Typography by Larissa Lawrynenko

1 2 3 4 5 6 7 8 9 10

First Edition

to those who sacrifice for their families

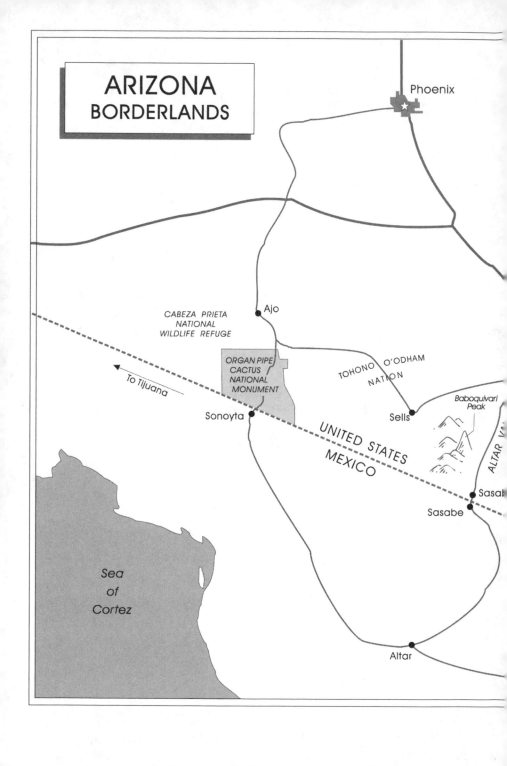

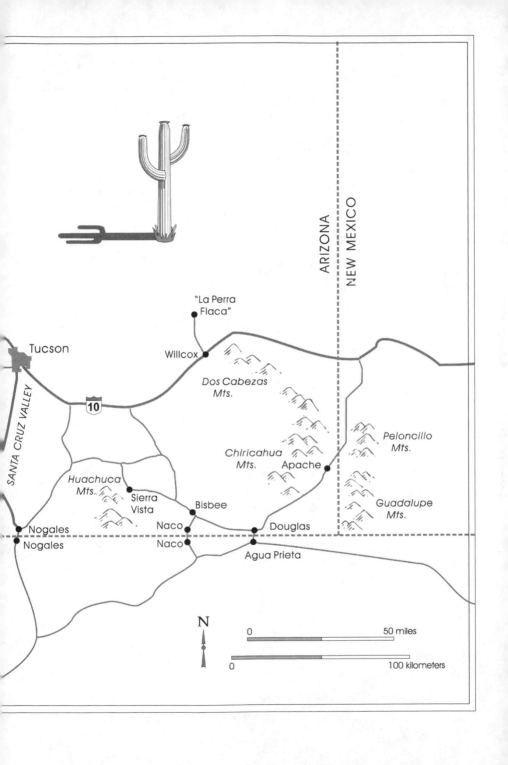

"La Perra Flaca"

Tucson

Willcox

Dos Cabezas Mts.

SANTA CRUZ VALLEY

10

Chiricahua Mts.

Apache

Peloncillo Mts.

Huachuca Mts.

Sierra Vista

Bisbee

Guadalupe Mts.

Nogales
Nogales

Naco
Naco

Douglas

Agua Prieta

ARIZONA

NEW MEXICO

N

0   50 miles

0   100 kilometers

Old Friends

THE END WAS COMING, but I didn't see it coming.

I was done for the day. The sun had set, my shovel was on my shoulder, and I was walking up the path to the village. As I passed under a high stone wall, my mind only on my empty stomach, a shadowy figure swooped down on me with a shriek that could have raised the dead. I let out a yelp and leaped out of the way.

"Scared you," cried my best friend, Rico Rivera. "Scared you bad, Victor Flores."

I shook my shovel at him. "'Mano, you're lucky I didn't attack you with this."

"What did you think I was?"

"A flying cow, you maniac."

"You should have heard yourself! You squealed like a pig!"

I could only laugh. It had been a long time since Rico had pulled a trick like this. This was the way it used to be with Rico and me, until three years ago, when Rico started trade school in the city of Silao. He lived there now with his sister, whose husband worked at the General Motors plant. Sometimes Rico came home to the village on weekends, but I wouldn't always see him. We were fifteen years old now, with life pulling us in different directions, but we still called each other 'mano. We were hermanos in our hearts. Actual brothers couldn't have grown up much closer.

Rico put his arm around my shoulder. "I have something to tell you, Victor." Suddenly he wasn't joking around. "Follow me," Rico said gravely. "I have a secret to show you."

"You know how I hate secrets. I thought there weren't any between us."

"A couple of minutes, and there won't be."

Dusk was deepening as Rico led me past the village church, past the cemetery and the dirt field where we'd played fútbol and béisbol ever since I could remember. I followed my friend to the old village, abandoned after an earthquake hundreds of years before. All that remained, overgrown with brush, vines, and cactus, were the stone walls built to hold back the hillside. The moon was up, but its light was weak and eerie. This was a place to stay away from.

Rico paused where one of these ancient walls was especially thick with giant prickly pear. "We have to crawl underneath the cactus," he announced.

I wasn't so sure.

"It should be easy for you, Victor. C'mon, Tortuga."

Only Rico called me Turtle. It was a little joke of his. With his long legs, he'd always been the better sprinter, but not by much. "Turtle," though, was only partly about running. Mostly it had to do with my cautiousness.

Here and now, I had reason to be cautious. This was where my four sisters collected cactus fruit and also the pads for roasting as nopales. Teresa, the oldest of my sisters, always carried a stick on account of the rattlesnakes.

Unlike Rico, I was afraid of rattlesnakes. "It's too murky to be crawling in there," I told him.

"I know what you're afraid of, but it's the middle of March. They haven't come out yet. Just follow me."

As always, Rico went first. Once inside, we sat next to each other, our backs to the ancient wall. "Just like the old days," Rico said.

I liked hearing him say that, but it wasn't like Rico to be sentimental. What was this all about? Maybe it was going to be a trick after all. There would be no secret.

"Watch this," Rico said as he reached into a crevice and brought out a small glass jar. With a gleam in his eye, he placed it in my hand. In the patchy moonlight, I had to bring the jar close to my face to make out what was inside. It was a roll of money, and not pesos. American greenbacks, with the number 100 showing. "How much?" I gasped.

"There are fifteen of those. You're looking at one thousand, five hundred American dollars."

I was astounded. In school I had learned to convert kilos to pounds and kilometers to miles. But pesos to dollars was different,

3

floating up and down. The last I heard, it was eleven to one. That meant this was more than sixteen thousand pesos. My family could get by for more than a year on this much money. "I don't understand," I said. "Your parents gave it to you?"

"My parents? Did you hit your head, 'mano?"

"Did you win the lottery? Is the money yours, Rico?"

"It's mine. It's from one of my brothers in the States. It's my coyote money."

The expression meant only one thing. Coyotes were the smugglers who took people across the border to El Norte.

It didn't seem possible. "You're leaving for the other side?"

"Yes, I'm leaving Mexico. I'm going to cross the wire. Destination, the United States of America."

This Is My Chance

RICO TWIRLED HIS MONEY jar in the moonlight. "In the last year, Victor, the price that the coyotes charge to get you across the border has gone from a thousand dollars to fifteen hundred. And here it is, fifteen hundred."

"It's not only more expensive," I said, "it's more difficult and dangerous. It must be really bad. From the whole village, only four men came home this winter."

"I know. When they leave, they're taking me with them. It's going to be exciting. Fortino, the leader, says we might have to try a couple of times before we make it across. I'll make it, no problem—I'm a fast runner."

Rico wanted me to be excited for him. How could I pretend I was? It was all too much: this fortune in bills to be handed over to the smugglers, and even more so, the danger Rico thought was so appealing.

"I'm not afraid," he insisted.

"You should be."

"It's different for you, Victor, because of what happened to your father. I understand. He was unlucky, that's all."

This hurt. My father had traveled back and forth across the wire many times, working in El Norte and returning to the family for only a few precious months every winter. Four years ago, he returned home in a coffin. He had always worked in the fields and the orchards, but this time he had taken a job helping to build the foundation for a new high school in the state of South Carolina. When the accident happened, my father and a friend from the village were doing some shovel work in a deep, sandy trench. With no warning, the walls collapsed on them. Both of them were killed.

"Why do you think you will be lucky?" I asked. "What about the desert? Every day, it is said, people die in the desert."

"That may be true, but think how many get through to shake the hand of Mickey Mouse."

Rico was smiling at his little joke. I was still too stunned to laugh. "Don't be so serious, Victor. Once I get across the border, it's the land of opportunity. Everyone agrees, everything's better in the States. It's not like I'm making this all up. A teacher from my school quit two weeks ago to go work at a Laundromat in Los Angeles."

Rico knew a lot about El Norte. Ever since I could remember, he liked everything American—cars, music, fashions. His hair was cut short and bleached the same yellow as his Lakers cap.

"You said your brother gave you this money. Which brother?"

"Reynaldo, the oldest. He wired it to a Western Union in Silao, in care of Fortino."

Rico was the last of eleven children, the baby of his family. He'd come along like a miracle after his brothers and sisters had already left home. Most of them lived and worked in the States, but his parents allowed no contact. As Rico had often told me, they were afraid he would run off to join them.

"Isn't Reynaldo the one your father never even speaks of?"

"I guess they never got along. Reynaldo is the one with the most money. He takes care of people's swimming pools in Tucson. Reynaldo even has one of his own — imagine that! He has another business, too, buying and selling cars."

Rico always spoke of cars with reverence, even in front of his father, who couldn't afford one. Nobody in Los Árboles could, and the same went for tractors. Ours was a village with so little that it didn't even have the trees it was named after.

"You've told your parents," I said.

"Are you crazy? I can't tell them."

"When are you leaving?"

"Tomorrow! March is the best time, before the desert gets hot."

I felt queasy. Rico had grown up knowing he was supposed to stay home, nearby, like his sister in Silao. If he did well at the technical school, he would be able to get a job where his brother-in-law worked, putting together the Suburbans at the General Motors plant. His parents were counting on him to look after them in their old age. I had heard Rico's mother say these things more times than I could remember.

No, I shouldn't have been surprised about Rico leaving for the States. Rico wanted all the things that money could buy. But just as much, it was the adventure he was after.

I didn't know what to say. I had no desire to go to the other side. Living in El Norte had been the dream of my family a long time ago, but that dream died even before my father did. It had become too expensive and too dangerous to sneak an entire family across.

Rico twirled his money jar and said, "Things are complicated in my house, not simple like in yours, Victor."

I didn't want to argue, not now. Things were not simple for my family, they were scary. Rico knew I had to raise a crop of corn to sell every year, but he didn't know that the little money my father had left behind was long gone, and the price of corn kept falling like a crippled bird. Rico didn't know we were teetering on the brink of disaster. My sisters' hand-me-down clothes were practically in tatters. No toys for my little brother. And Rico didn't know what it felt like to be hungry, really hungry, the way we had been this winter. Turning the soil these last few weeks, sometimes I got so light-headed I thought I would faint.

I hadn't been able to talk to Rico about these things before, and I couldn't bring myself to do it now. "Have you even met your oldest brother?" I asked.

"He was here once when I was little, but I don't remember him."

"If he doesn't even know you, why would he give you the coyote money?"

"Because I asked him for it. I wrote to him. I told him I wanted to work, that I'd help clean the swimming pools, wash cars, do anything."

"How could you write to him? How did you know where to write?"

8

"I found a letter from him, to my parents. They never showed it to me. I found it in a chest at home."

"Why didn't you tell me?"

"I didn't even get the money until last week. There was no time to tell you. And now I have to go, and go soon."

"Why is that?"

"Haven't you heard? The Americans are talking about letting everybody work legally—everybody who is already there. But you have to get across now, as soon as you can. Once you're a legal worker, it's only a matter of time before they change the law some more, and allow you to become a citizen. That's what everyone thinks is going to happen."

"Rico, I just don't see how you're going to tell your parents."

"I didn't say I was," he snapped. "I would if I could, Victor! But if I tell them, they won't let me go—you know that. 'Mano, they'll never forgive me for doing this, but I'll never forgive myself if I don't."

"You can't leave like a thief in the night, without their blessing."

"I won't have to go in the night. My parents are going into Silao tomorrow on the morning bus. I'll take the afternoon bus."

I bit my tongue to hold back words that should never be spoken between friends.

"Do you think this is easy for me?" Rico said. "My heart is breaking."

"Don't go, then. You still have time to reconsider."

"Believe me, that's all I've been doing. This is my chance! You should be happy for me!"

"I'm afraid for you."

"Victor, you are my best friend. After I leave, I want you to tell my parents."

"Me? How can I?"

"You'll be able to say that you didn't know, that I didn't tell you either, not until the last minute."

"What if it doesn't work out about the swimming pools?"

"I'll work in the fields, whatever it takes."

"You hate working in the fields!"

A silence grew between us as I thought about Rico's parents, and the danger. To my surprise, my friend began sobbing.

My childhood had ended when my father died, when I left the village school and began to work in the fields. Rico's ended when this idea had taken root in his mind.

Rico wiped away the tears and said, "I'm going."

I reached for my friend and embraced him. If he had to stay home against his will, he was going to be like a lion in a cage. I tried to speak but found it impossible.

"I will miss you," I finally managed. "Very much."

"Ask my parents to forgive me, Victor."

"I will. Will I ever see you again, Rico?"

"Who can say? Whatever happens, you'll always be my brother, even if you are a turtle."

Through the sting of my own tears, I said farewell. "Travel well, my brother."

Trouble of My Own

L OS ÁRBOLES IS AN out-of-the-way place surrounded by mountains. From the village, it's a walk of a mile to reach the back road that runs between Guanajuato, the beautiful city of old churches, and Silao, the not-so-beautiful city of auto plants. Silao is closer, and that's where people from the village go to shop. Los Árboles has only one small store for things like candy, sodas, and lottery tickets. This Saturday morning, there were many people walking the dirt track through the fields to catch the bus.

Hoping to avoid Rico's parents, I kept my eyes on my shovel work. There was still a chance Rico would change his mind, and I would not have to tell them the news that would break their hearts. Keep working, I told myself. Think only about the crop you'll soon be planting.

The only answer I knew to the falling price of corn was to plant more corn. In addition to my family's plot, I was tilling two pieces of ground long gone to weeds. They didn't belong to us, but that was okay. Most of the fields lay fallow, abandoned by men working in El Norte or by families who had left for the cities—usually Querétaro or Mexico City.

I knew why Señor Rivera was going into Silao, but I couldn't guess what would take Rico's mother away with her son home for the weekend, unless it was shopping for the makings of a special dinner for him.

It was impossible to think of Rico's parents without remembering their kindness. Ten years before, when my father knocked on their door, the Riveras opened it to complete strangers. The rain forest of Chiapas, close by the Guatemala border, was where we actually were from, a land of monkeys and parrots, giant snakes and jaguars, poverty and violence. My parents had been caught up in the struggle of the poor to grow crops on land that belonged to the wealthy. In the end, we had to flee for our lives, and were trying to reach the United States. We made it halfway when my father was robbed by a pickpocket at the bus station in Silao.

A priest from Silao gave my father a little money and put us on a bus heading for the city of Guanajuato, with instructions for the driver to let us off at the path to Los Árboles. We would know we were on the right track if we were walking toward the outstretched hands of El Cristo Rey, the gigantic statue of Christ the King that crowns the summit of the mountain above the village. The priest told my father to go find Señor Emilio Rivera, who was a leader in his village and a friend to strangers. That was Rico's father. We have lived here ever since.

"Victor! Victor!" A familiar voice was calling my name and bringing me back to the present. Rico's father was motioning to me. He was wearing his best going-to-town jeans and a clean shirt. His black felt cowboy hat over his thick silver hair made him look even more dignified than usual.

Señora Rivera, also dressed up, went ahead slowly with one of her friends.

Señor Rivera limped toward me. Pangs of guilt and shame ran through me for the terrible secret I was keeping. Had Rico been able to sleep? I'd woken exhausted, as if all night I'd been wrestling a wild beast. I ran to meet the old man, to save him the trouble. His limp was from the tractor accident in Colorado that ended his migrations. He had worked in El Norte for almost thirty years, though not since Rico was a small child.

"I only have a minute," Señor Rivera said. "At the house, I've sharpened a shovel. You're welcome to borrow it. Trade for a day, and I'll sharpen yours."

I thanked him. Rico's father was proud to be a campesino, a true man of the countryside. He had a great love for the village and wanted to believe that there was still a future for farming in Los Árboles. He had started the village co-op a few years before when the price of corn started the slide that wasn't over yet. The co-op was so the growers could sell their crops all together and get a better price than they would if they sold small amounts by themselves.

"This evening I will bring back the news from the meeting of the co-ops," Señor Rivera said, "about the outlook for the prices this year."

I wiped sweat from my eyes and said, "I will be saying my prayers."

Midday came, and I left the field for our comida. Three of my sisters were already at the table. Mamá called from her outdoor oven. Our little brother, Chuy, ran to open the door for her, his eyes big as our empty plates, ever hopeful for a miracle of loaves and fishes.

The platter of tortillas and the bowl of rice and beans were going to make a meager meal. As my mother set the food down, I grappled with my feelings. I was the man of the family. I should have been able to provide better than this.

Graciela joined us from behind one of the blankets hanging over the openings of the two small bedrooms. "Who took my lipstick?" she cried. The youngest of the girls, Graciela was nine and very protective of her birthday present.

Little Chuy bugged out his eyes and puckered his lips like a fish. They were bright red.

Graciela got a look on her face, and was about to reach for Chuy. Mamá saw this coming, bowed her head, and began to say the grace, which she added onto at the end. She said that the last night of frost was coming soon. This year we would plant an especially big garden. By the middle of April, we would have fresh greens.

"Pepe de Chu-ey!" Graciela cried as soon as Mamá was finished. "Where did you put it?"

"On my lips," the chango said, with his monkey grin.

"Give it back!" She lunged for his pockets but he darted away.

"Enough," Mamá said. "Sit down, both of you."

"Chuy," Graciela hissed. "I'll get you later."

Mamá served me first, with Teresa, Mari Cruz, Isabel, Graciela, and little Chuy looking on. Chuy was short for Jesús. His baptismal name was José de Jesús. Sometimes we called him by both nicknames—Pepe de Chuy.

My sisters and brother watched Mamá pack my tortilla half full of beans and rice, then place a bowl of rice with milk in front of me. It was left over from my early meal, before the others were even awake. "Something extra for all that hard digging the rest of the day," she said to me, but it was more for the others, especially Chuy, who was born with three stomachs.

I gave my bowl of rice with milk to my brother, who hadn't yet learned to hide his hunger. Mamá disapproved, Graciela groaned. I couldn't help it. Seeing my little brother hungry always felt like a knife turning in my heart. He was only five years old.

I went back to work. An hour later my mother, sisters, and Chuy came down to the field. They broke up the clods behind me and raked the earth smooth as they had been doing weekday afternoons. When the time came for hoeing the weeds, and finally for harvesting, I would need their help with that, also.

By late afternoon I was alone again and keeping my eye on the path. This time I was working in the plot farthest from it. If Rico was going to pass by with the men who were leaving, I didn't want to be close enough to see his face or have him see mine. I busied myself slinging rocks off the field and worrying about the price I would get when the time came to sell this year's corn. The price had to go up this summer, it just *had* to. We needed the cash money, and more than we made last year—real money to buy all the things we couldn't keep going without. If the news Señor Rivera brought home this evening was bad, I didn't know what we were going to do. It was me who should be going north, not Rico.

At the time of last summer's disappointment, I tried to get Rico's father to explain why the prices kept going down every year. "Here is the reason," Señor Rivera said with his voice beginning to tremble. "All over Mexico, people are buying less and less of our own corn for cornmeal. American corn is cheaper. Mexican corn is heading for the edge of the cliff."

None of this made sense to me, but I never got more of an explanation. The subject made Rico's father very upset.

From the corner of my eye I saw a group of men walking toward the road to catch the afternoon bus to Silao. These were the men leaving for El Norte. Were there four, or were there five? The way they were bunched up, I couldn't tell. Was Rico with them or not?

No family members kept them company on their way to the bus. That was the custom. There was too much sadness about the leaving. Good-byes were said at home, behind closed doors.

I took a long look. I tried to make out something that would identify my friend. The sun caught some short yellow hair showing under a yellow baseball cap. It was Rico.

4

The Bells of Los Árboles

I WATCHED THE BUS DISAPPEAR, and with it my best friend. There was nothing to do but put my foot to my shovel.

It was tough digging. The soil had to be freed from the roots of the weeds, and the winter frosts had brought rocks to the surface. I kept at it until the sun was low in the sky, until I saw the late bus from Silao returning.

The village bells were tolling, possibly to mark the return of the bus. Old Carmita, who lived close by the church, rang them for any and all occasions, real and imagined. She had rung them at the funeral of my father as he was lowered into the ground behind the church. After that, the bells always made me uneasy. As people stepped off the bus and started up the path, I felt light-headed, weak all over. How was I going to tell Rico's parents that he had run away?

I felt almost paralyzed as the villagers drew closer, among them the proud man with the black hat and silver hair. It was Señor Rivera who had spoken up for me when the teacher in the village school wasn't going to let me enroll without a birth certificate. Señor Rivera had been like a second father to me. The idea of telling Rico's mother was even more terrifying. All those years she had welcomed me into her beautiful home, a dark-faced Indian kid from Chiapas who lived on dirt floors and without electricity. Fed me, encouraged me, told me how smart I was.

What was I going to say to them?

As the people got closer and began to pass by, I went back to work, hoping Rico's parents would also pass by. Instead, I heard my name called. I walked toward Rico's father with no idea how I was going to find the words to tell him about his son.

This time Rico's mother wasn't walking ahead. She was staying at her husband's side. This was going to make it worse, far worse.

As I drew close, it was easy to see that Señor Rivera was very upset. He and his wife appeared to be holding each other up. "I'm sorry, Victor," Rico's father began. "The news is a catastrophe. A big meeting of the countries has been held. The Americans wouldn't even budge."

"I don't understand."

"They say that 'free trade' is supposed to help us. We get manufacturing jobs like my son-in-law's at the General Motors plant in Silao. That's fine with the American companies. It's expensive for them to pay car workers in the States. But when it comes to agriculture, this free trade is killing us. This year is going to be no different, after all. The Americans refuse to stop selling their cheap corn in Mexico."

I went weak in the knees. "How could American corn be cheaper than ours? The Americans have to send theirs here, and just to grow it up there must cost a lot of money. All those tractors, all that fuel—"

"Chemical fertilizers, pesticides . . ." Señor Rivera agreed.

"How much do I spend? How can they grow corn cheaper than I can?"

"They can't grow it cheaper," Rico's father replied angrily. "The only way those big farmers up there can make a profit is because the government gives them a lot of money in addition to what they get when they sell their corn. Subsidies, they call it."

"But why would their government do that?"

"So their farmers can make a profit! To keep them in business!"

"Don't they know it will put us *out* of business?"

"They know." The veins were standing out on Señor Rivera's forehead. His face was very red. "More and more people from Mexico will try to cross the border now, to find work. This, while the Americans are trying harder than ever to turn us back, ever since the terrorist attacks."

Rico's mother had been waiting for the conversation to be over. She looked very tired. "My wife has been to the clinic," Señor Rivera said. "We should be getting home."

"So, what should I do, Señor Rivera? What should I do?"

"You might as well not plant any corn, Victor—no more than

your family can eat. It's not going to get better this year. In fact, it's going to get much worse. If you are able to sell your corn at all, you will get almost nothing for it. They might not even come to buy it this year. I'm sorry."

The old couple turned away, and I let them go. I would tell them about Rico later. Anytime would be better than now.

For the moment, I put thoughts of my friend aside. I was scared to death. *If you are able to sell your corn at all, you will get almost nothing for it.* What would happen to my family? What was I going to do?

I turned my back on the field and stumbled home, my head wrapped in storm clouds. I was cornered now, and my mind was racing for a way out. Somehow, somewhere, I had to find work that would pay cash money.

It was impossible to live in the village and work in Silao. Should I leave the village, try to live in Silao? No chance I could get work at the auto plants, with no training, no experience. Could I try to find work fixing tires, something like that? Even if I could, it wouldn't pay enough, not to support my whole family.

It was clear as can be, what I somehow had to do. Only in El Norte could I earn enough money soon enough. But how could I get across without coyote money? Without paying the smugglers, was it even possible? I hurried home, trembling at the idea that I might have to try it anyway. How I envied Rico his fifteen hundred dollars.

My sisters and brother were away hauling water and scavenging firewood to cook the next few meals. "What's the matter?" my mother asked as soon as she saw my face. "What happened?"

At first I told her about Rico, what he had done. I said I would tell his parents in the morning.

My mother shook her head. "You must tell them tonight."

I took a deep breath. "There's something worse," I said, and went on to break the news about our corn.

My mother listened all the way through with her hand to her chin. Afterward she didn't speak. This was a crushing blow.

"What can we do, Mamá?"

"We won't be able to get through another winter. We will have to leave."

"Where will we go—Silao?"

She hesitated. "We might be able to survive in Guanajuato."

I knew what this meant. My mother had mentioned this possibility to me once before. Guanajuato was very popular with tourists, especially the Americans. They loved the hilly city's cobbled streets, brightly colored houses, and old Spanish buildings. It was possible for people with no homes and no work to survive there by begging along the streets that led to the beautiful churches. I had seen this with my own eyes.

To picture my mother huddled on the sidewalk all day long, her hand held out and her eyes on the ground, made me turn myself inside out with exasperation. What would become of my sisters? Of my little brother?

I thought of my father. I was glad such a picture had never

entered his mind. "Not Guanajuato," I said.

"Where else is there to turn?"

"El Norte."

"But we can't all—"

"Just me, Mamá."

Her face fell. "Don't even suggest it."

"It's time for me to go work in El Norte, like Papá did. Send money home like he did. It's time for me to do what men from the village have to do."

"I would never ask this of you. You've heard the talk. It's worse than ever on the border. Anyway, we have no money for you to pay the coyotes. Your father always had to pay the coyotes."

"There must be people who make it across on their own."

"Too risky, too dangerous. You never hear of them."

"I'll find them, and tag along. And I'll find work, somehow."

My mother placed her hands on my shoulders. "Don't you understand, my son? Even if you were able to cross the desert and find work, you would always be among strangers, and living in the fear of being deported. And what about us? We also would be living in fear, not knowing how you are doing, hearing nothing at all, not even that you are alive. Your father's letters never even got to the village."

"If only the store had a telephone."

"Don't begin with 'if only.' If only this, if only that, if only your father hadn't died. That kind of thinking will make you sick."

"I would wire money to the Western Union in the bank in Silao, like Papá did, and you would go once a month on the bus to see if it arrived. Then you would know I was okay."

"That would be all we had of you, some money."

"A *lot* of money. Enough to buy food for yourself and Chuy and the girls. To buy clothes and all the other things that they need, buy gifts for their birthdays and Christmas. If I do well in the States, there will be enough money for Teresa and Mari Cruz to go to school in Silao. You know how much they want to keep going to school. There's nothing for them in the village."

My mother touched my face with both her hands, gentle despite their roughness. Then she let go. "I've thought about El Norte myself. I've heard stories of mothers who have made the crossing. They work in the restaurants up there, or in the hotels, and send money home to children who are lost to them. I could never bring myself to try it."

"Thank God," I said. "Mamá, it's up to me. It's my time. You understand, don't you?"

"You wouldn't leave without my blessing, would you, like Rico?"

"I couldn't, but please listen. . . . What else can we do?"

She closed her eyes, gathered herself. I felt the pain that came with being a mother. At last she looked at me again, and she spoke, this time with a note of acceptance in her voice. "Tomorrow, you should go up to El Cristo Rey to pray and think. I'll talk to the Virgin of Guadalupe. She listens to the poor and the desperate."

5

A Bitter Sweetness

I STAYED AWAY FROM THE FOLDS of the mountain, where brush choked the ravines. The slopes I was climbing were steep and mostly bare. The hike to El Cristo Rey usually took three hours. Today, knowing I might be leaving, I stopped along the way to appreciate the greening valley and the surrounding mountains.

Rico's father once told me that our side of the mountain used to be covered with pine forests. The Spanish cut them down to use in the mines and to build the cities. The land has been drying up ever since.

I wondered if these things could be true. Rico's father carried grudges, against the Americans and even the Spanish of hundreds of years before, who must have been his ancestors, in part if not mostly. I asked my mother once if any of our ancestors were Spaniards. She didn't think so. She said we were Tojolabal, descendants of the Maya.

I was grateful that Rico's parents weren't going to hold a grudge against me for last evening, for telling them what Rico had done. It had been terrible, trying to find the words to tell them, terrible what the words had done to them. Rico's mother gave one sharp cry, and then she was speechless. I saw the color go from her face and hope from her eyes.

They believed me when I explained that Rico had told me only the night before. They didn't even blame me for not warning them. "Working with his brother, that will come to grief sooner or later," Rico's father said at the door.

"But why?" I asked.

"Because Reynaldo lacks honesty. I told him as much once to his face, which is why he has done this. To spite me."

The door groaned on its hinges shutting behind me. From now on, the house of the Riveras was going to be a sad and lonely place.

The tolling of the village bells, carrying far up the slopes, brought me back to my feet. I climbed higher until Los Árboles was like a toy village and the road from Guanajuato to Silao shrank to a ribbon. I sat down again and took it in once more, the world I had known. Even with the forest missing, it was beautiful.

It was home. All I remembered of the forests of Chiapas was their emerald green color, and the jaguar. The great spotted cat had come to the edge of the forest and looked at me one day as I was playing on the grass behind our house with its roof of thatch. I was too young to even be afraid.

When I was older, and told my father of this memory, he didn't say I had imagined it. Papá told me that our ancestors had built some of their greatest temples to the tigre. The powers of other animals didn't even come close.

Nearing the top, I spiraled around the summit of El Cubilete, the Tumbler, until I reached the road, which was jammed with cars, taxis, and tour buses creeping into the parking lot. I hurried to get past the diesel fumes. Inside the horseshoe-shaped shrine, the plaza was crowded with pilgrims of all ages. Many were on their knees, with eyes lifted to the sky and the gigantic statue of bronze.

I was disappointed to find it so crowded. It was a Sunday, but Easter was still a month away. I wasn't even going to try to get into the chapel. Stepping to the side, I took a long look at El Cristo Rey standing atop the chapel's roof, rounded to represent the top half of the world. One of the angels at His feet offered the crown of a king, the other a crown of thorns. I felt sorry for Him. Christ the King, with arms outstretched, had too many prayers to listen to. It wasn't like my family was the only one in trouble.

I had to get away from the crush, yet I wanted to stay close by awhile, someplace where I could do my thinking. I found it on a low concrete wall next to a bus from Mexico City. From my perch I could see Los Árboles, and think about what I had to do. The noise behind me wouldn't matter.

When my mind cleared, I saw my path. We didn't have another choice. Somehow, I had to make the journey north. For my father, for the family. I had to find work. I had to send the money home.

From out of nowhere, a figure in black sat down next to me, an old priest. "Do you mind if I sit down?"

"Please, padre."

"One of the great statues of the world," the priest began. "I suppose you know why it was erected here."

"The top of El Cubilete is at the exact center of all the land in Mexico."

"You are very bright."

"Well, I learned it in school."

"Where are you from?"

I pointed. "That village way down there."

"Not big enough to have a priest?"

"Once a month."

The priest's eyes went from Los Árboles to my hands, rough as the skin of an iguana, and back to the village again. "I've been watching you. You seem to have the weight of the world on your shoulders."

"That's almost what it feels like," I admitted.

"Your father is no doubt working in El Norte."

Uncomfortably, I nodded my head. I didn't like to tell the story of my father. I didn't want sympathy.

"With so many men away," the priest said with a sigh, "it's as if the villages of Mexico are filled with widows and orphans."

As we spoke, the bus had been filling with passengers returning from the shrine. As the last few boarded, the priest got up to join them and pressed something into my hand. I saw that it was some peso bills.

"The people on the bus gave me this for talking to them on the way here," the padre explained. "No doubt your mother needs it more than I do. And by the way, it appears to me that you have very strong shoulders."

I thanked him, and said that I would remember him. I watched the bus go, and then I started down the mountain. It wasn't long before I stopped to count the money. I was surprised when I found out how much it was. It might even be enough to take me to the border.

As I ran down the mountain, a dust devil was whirling in my mind. "Bus money!" I began by announcing. I showed my mother the bills and told her how I had come by them.

My mother crossed herself. Her eyes were large as ten-peso coins. "Surely this is a sign. Twice, a priest has given us bus money. Praise be to God and His blessed mother."

"I should leave soon, before the deserts get too hot."

"I understand. Your father always left by now."

"I guess I should leave tomorrow."

It pained my mother too much to reply with more than a nod.

"I'll go through Guadalajara, like he did. And cross in Arizona, like he did."

I went to the creek with a bar of soap, washed my hair and scrubbed my skin raw. The bathing pool was in the shadows. The cold water felt like the stings of a thousand scorpions. I was filled with doubts. Was I brave enough to go through with this? How was my family going to manage without me? What if it didn't rain, and the barrels that collected water from the roof remained empty? Our family used to have a burro to haul clean water from upstream, but we traded it for the milk goat. I wished I'd dug a new pit for the outhouse. Now my sisters would have to do that.

As I returned from the creek I saw my little brother waving from the rooftop. The entire family was waiting. During the summer, we watched the sunset together from the roof. It was always cooler up there. On the fourteenth of March, there was a cold wind blowing. I climbed the ladder to join them.

Lined up on the bench, facing the great statue, we watched our last sunset together. My mother had put on her finery from Chiapas: her blouse embroidered with many colors, and her long black skirt. This was all so out of the ordinary, it was more than a little scary for my sisters and little Chuy.

"Victor is leaving in the morning for El Norte," Mamá began. "To find work, for the sake of the family, like your father used to do."

"Will he be back for Christmas?" Chuy asked, as if I was already gone.

"Chuy," Graciela said. "Victor might not be back for years."

Chuy broke into tears and held tight to his mother. My sisters were trying to be brave. Teresa, the oldest, gave me a look of such pride I will remember it as long as I live.

My eyes went to the summit high above. The sunset was over. El Cristo Rey was a silhouette against a band of violet surrendering to black.

Chuy usually slept beside me on the floor, on the mattress we shared. Not this night. I heard my little brother cry himself to sleep in the next room with his mother and his sisters.

Never in my life had I felt so alone. Unlike Rico, I wasn't a brave person. I had no desire for adventure.

With the leaving so close, I couldn't sleep. I sat at the kitchen table with my head in my hands.

After awhile my mother appeared at the doorway. "I can't sleep, Mamá."

"Neither can I. Let us keep each other company while we still can. I've been lying awake thinking that I should have made you some hot chocolate. Now I have another chance. Would you like that?"

"Very much."

We pulled on warm clothes and went outside. I started a fire in the stove of mud and cement my father had made. My mother heated the milk slowly, breaking off the last pieces of the hard chocolate. It was expensive, for special occasions only. Slowly, slowly, she kept stirring as the chocolate dissolved. At the last, she twirled the molinillo stick between her palms to make the froth.

She took the pot off and let the mixture cool. All the while, the half moon and stars were wheeling. I wished I could stop them. It was impossible to find the right words to say.

My mother poured the hot chocolate into our cups. "It's good," I said.

"Yes, but with a bitter sweetness tonight, my son."

"Now that the time is so close, Mamá, I am so unsure. I have to go, but I don't know where I will find the strength, and the courage."

She touched her heart. "In the part of you that is always home, no matter where you are. Think of us, and it will help. Always know, you are never alone."

"How long can you hold out here without money arriving?"

"We can sell the goat and the chickens. We can get by on the garden until the first frost, around the Day of the Dead. Once it freezes, that would be the end."

In the morning, my family didn't walk with me. Inside the house, they emptied out their tears as I walked the long silent mile to the bus alone. It was a cloudy day, and I was shivering under my jacket. The village bells began to toll. The sound reminded me of the day my father was lowered into the ground. I wished I had thought to visit his grave before setting out.

The bus was pulling up. I had told myself that I wasn't going to look back at the village, but I couldn't help it. When I did, I felt as weak as an old cornstalk rattling in the winds of winter.

6

The Lone Wolf

THE BUS STATION IN SILAO was crowded. Remembering what had happened to my father here, years before, I kept a good grip on my shoulder bag. What little money I had was stuffed in my underwear. I tried to look unafraid, as if I knew what I was doing. All the while, I felt like a bird out of the nest before it was ready to fly.

I counted five different groups of travelers in the station. Many of them wore straw hats like mine, sneakers like mine. I wondered how many were campesinos, and leaving their fields for the first time. Most carried small nylon backpacks, which meant they were headed for the States. Like me, they were waiting for the bus to Guadalajara.

I wondered if any of these men had one of those famous green cards the Americans gave so few of. My father never had one, and neither did Rico's. Without a green card, you were illegal on the other side. You were a mojado—a wetback—as my father had often called himself. He said that the name came from swimming across the Rio Grande River into Texas, but really it meant all the illegal workers, even if they crossed on dry land.

Probably all these men were going to be mojados—"wets"— same as me. The difference between us was the coyote money they had on them, American dollars earned in the States, big money like Rico was carrying three days ago when he passed through here with the group from Los Árboles.

How I wished I was traveling with a group of experienced men. All Rico had to do was follow along, and when the time came, pull out his money to pay the coyote who would smuggle them across.

Without staring at the men in the station, I was looking them over carefully. I had to find an ally, someone else in my situation. There had to be people like me, who had to go north but didn't have coyote money. It only made sense that they wouldn't band together and make a group. A man alone, or maybe two, would have a much better chance of sneaking through.

At last I spotted a man with a small backpack who entered the station by himself, bought a ticket, and stood alone. If he was head-ing north, here was someone I should keep an eye on.

The man was taller than average, lean as a fencepost, about thirty. No doubt he'd made many crossings. Experience lay heavy on him, like a tree much carved upon. His shaggy hair, drooping mus-tache, and downcast eyes—one with a sleepy eyelid—made him look like someone to stay away from, a lone wolf kicked out of the pack. A lone wolf was what I was looking for, but this one I was in no hurry to meet.

My bus was called. I went out to the platform and lined up. Several of the mojado groups were getting on this bus, and so was Sleepy Eye.

As I boarded, I was amazed by the plush seats with high backs and headrests, and by the air-conditioning. My mother had told me that the first class buses would be the quickest and safest way to go. It was how my father had traveled to the Arizona border.

Stay alert, I told myself as I started down the aisle. I noticed that the mojados were putting their backpacks in the overhead compartment opposite the seat they were choosing. To keep an eye on their things, most likely. I would do the same. Two-thirds of the way back, I came to the first open seats. My lone wolf was on the aisle. I stowed my bag above him, ducked into the row directly across, and sat at the window. I had to keep track of him, just in case he turned out to be the one.

The bus pulled out of the station and left Silao behind. Out the window, I was looking over the horizon of my world. From here on, every single city and town, every mountain and valley, was going to be new and strange. It was exciting, but even more, it was scary.

Once on the open road, the bus went much faster than the buses I was used to. The ride was smoother and quieter. The driver had the radio tuned to the powerful signal of Radio XEG, La Ranchera de Monterrey. I loved ranchera music, the stories that the songs told, the dramatic, emotional singing. Rico couldn't stand ranchera, especially the mariachis. I pictured him pulling out his headphones and turning up the volume on his own music.

After a brief stop at Salamanca, we were on our way again. The song that was soon playing throughout the bus was the famous "Camino de Guanajuato." With the first notes, my heart swelled. It's the song of my tierra. The cities of Salamanca, León, and Dolores Hidalgo appear in it, and so does El Cristo Rey atop El Cubilete.

I looked around at the mojados surrounding me and found that I was not the only one dabbing at tears. Under the bill of his black baseball cap, even the eyes of the rough-looking lobo across the aisle looked moist. Rico thinks "Camino de Guanajuato" is ridiculously Mexican, dwelling as it does on the great sadness of life. At the end, the singer says he remains in his beloved town, but you can tell he is looking back with longing, and remains there only in his heart. It was almost too much to bear as I sped into the murky dusk and an even murkier future.

People talk of Guadalajara, a great city of beautiful churches. From the bus, in the dark, I didn't see any. At the city's huge terminal I threw my bag over my shoulder and lined up for my ticket for the next bus, which would take me all the way to the border city of Nogales. After paying, I was left with less than five dollars' worth of pesos. A man with no legs was selling plastic-coated pictures of Our Lady of Guadalupe. Of course I had to get one. I had no wallet to put it in, so I slipped it into the front pocket of my jeans.

Inside the Guadalajara terminal, there was not even room to sit on the floor. A good many of the throng were obviously mojados on the move. The place was so crowded, it was impossible to spot the men who were going north on their own, if there were any.

The departure board showed eleven buses heading for the border: six for Nogales, five for Tijuana. By chance, when my bus was called, my lobo also went out to the platform. I stayed close on his heels, telling myself I shouldn't be scared off by the weirdness of that sleepy eye. What if he turned out to be my only chance?

A third of the way back, he took an aisle seat on the left side. I stowed my bag and gathered my courage. "Sorry," I said, and squeezed by his knees, almost falling into the window seat. He gave me a look that said I was an idiot.

The bus filled up, and we took off. Several hours went by with only the thrum of the wheels below. No radio this time. People turned to the food they had brought aboard, talked quietly, or slept. I ate two of the tamales my mother had packed for me. Now and again, someone would go to the back of the bus. From my seat, I couldn't tell what they were doing. I got up the nerve to make conversation with Sleepy Eye. "Do you think the States will give everybody a green card and make us legal, like the rumors say?"

The man looked annoyed, but he answered. "Their President started the rumor, but I'll believe it when I see it."

I motioned over my shoulder. "What's in the back? Where are people going?"

He gave me that look again. "To the toilet."

"Oh," I said. "I've never been on a first-class bus before today."

He closed his eyes. This conversation was over. A couple hours went by. By this time I needed to go to the bathroom, but was afraid to squeeze by him.

It must have been the middle of the night when the driver braked so hard, it woke everyone up. Just ahead, police lights were flashing, lots of them. An accident, I guessed. My seatmate unsnapped his shirt pocket and took out what might have been a roll of money. He stuffed it in his underwear. "Roadblock," someone whispered. "Customs police."

I had never heard of customs police. I had no idea why they were stopping the traffic. It wasn't long before I found out.

A burly policeman in a tight, starched uniform boarded the bus. He said something to the driver. Bright lights came on, a shock to my eyes. The policeman glared down the aisle. The bus fell silent as the grave. His gun belt held a big pistol. "Passports, tourist cards, identification!"

My heart missed a beat, maybe two or three. I didn't have any of these things. "I've never carried identification before," I said to my lobo. "Do I need it?"

"I guess we'll find out," he said with a shrug.

"Is it against the law to travel without identification in your own country?"

"No, but this bus goes to the border."

"Who are they looking for?"

"Guatemalans, Hondurans, Salvadorans, Nicaraguans, South

Americans—anybody who doesn't have the proper documents to be in Mexico."

"Why do they care?"

"It makes the Americans happy."

By now the policeman was only three rows ahead. "People have told me I look Guatemalan," I said desperately.

"I'm not surprised."

"But I'm Mexican!"

"Don't tell me, tell him."

"What will they do?"

"Deport you to Guatemala, unless you are very lucky."

By this time I was terrified, and the customs policeman had arrived. My seatmate handed over his military registration card. I stared at it, wishing I had at least brought my father's. The policeman stared at the picture, then at the man, then at the picture. "Your name is Miguel Escobar."

"Yes."

"You are from the state of Guanajuato."

I almost answered before I realized that the policeman was still talking to this Miguel.

"Yes."

"What about this kid? Is he with you?"

"I don't know him."

"I am also from Guanajuato," I hurried to say. The words came out without enough breath. I sounded afraid.

"I didn't ask," the policeman said, taking a long, suspicious look at my Mayan face. A smile was growing at the corner of his mouth. He was happy. He had a mouse under his paw. "Very well, now is your turn. Passport!"

"No documents, but I am Mexican."

"Birth certificate!"

"I'm Mexican, born in Chiapas, close to the border with Guatemala."

"If I want a geography lesson, I will ask for it."

"I'm sorry," I said. "I can explain why I don't have a birth certificate. My father tried to get one for me when we still lived in Chiapas. He walked all the way to the town of La Realidad for it, but the office was closed."

The policeman looked as sympathetic as a snake about to strike. I hurried to explain that my family then moved to the state of Guanajuato when I was five. That I was from a village named Los Árboles located at the foot of El Cristo Rey.

"This will not do," the policeman snapped. "This proves nothing. Stand outside."

I sputtered, and pleaded, and almost cried.

"Outside!" he ordered.

7

No Turning Back

I GRABBED MY BAG AS I stumbled to the front of the bus. People turned their eyes away. Outside, a waiting policeman ordered me to stand at the rear of a pickup that had been pulled over, in the headlights of a police car behind it.

Two more customs police, one with an automatic rifle, were supervising a man unloading the heavy fruit and vegetable boxes stacked high in the cattle cage enclosing the bed of the truck. Skinny, uncombed, and more than a little nervous, this man was apparently the driver. The policeman with the assault rifle ordered me to help. "I'm not with him," I said. "I was on that bus."

"Do as I tell you," the policeman snarled. Pointing with his rifle, he ordered me to stack the boxes on the shoulder of the road. As the last ones came off the truck, I saw they'd been stacked on a deck of black plywood level with the tailgate, which was bolted shut.

Suddenly, from underneath the plywood, came a banging of metal on metal. Then more banging, along with cries and moans. There were people under there! Amid the confusion, the driver took off running. One policemen yelled at him, another fired bursts of bullets over his head. I got down on the ground, cringing like a dog. Nothing in my life had prepared me for this. It felt like I was in the middle of a war. The driver stopped in his tracks and held his hands high. They handcuffed him and threw him into one of the police cars.

I got up, still hoping to find a way back to the bus. The police removed the plywood and uncovered a terrible sight in the bed of the pickup: people writhing like snakes—men, women, and children. They had been packed in there like onions, side by side and head to foot.

"Yes, we are from Guatemala," I heard a man admit. One by one, they were helped out, thirteen of them. When they tried to stand up, most crumpled in pain to the ground as if they had no backbones. Their skin was dark, like mine, their faces round, their hair straight and black. I saw a catastrophe unfolding. I was going to be deported with them to Guatemala.

The police saw me trying to sidle away. They ordered me to get down with the others and I did. "I'm Mexican," I pleaded to the nearest man in uniform, towering above me. "I just got off that bus. I'm from near Silao. I'm Mexican, I promise. Ask me anything about Silao. Please, just let me go back home."

"Shut up!" the policeman barked. "Do what you are told!"

My bus, which had been idling, was now in gear. With a jerk of my head I saw the door closing, the bus pulling out.

Some of the Guatemalans, lying on their backs on the shoulder of the road, didn't even have the strength to sit up. "Who are you?" asked a small voice at my elbow, a boy Chuy's age. I didn't answer. My eyes were back on the police. For the time being, they weren't watching carefully.

All I knew was, I had to get away. I flipped over. Dragging my bag, I crawled under the front of the police car. One glance back, and I saw the boy staring at me. I had to pray he wouldn't say anything.

On my stomach, I bellied my way as far as the back wheels. No legs to be seen—I kept going. For a second, I crouched behind the police cruiser, then crept away, low and quiet as a cat. After a few minutes I heard shouts. By that time I was hundreds of yards away, racing down railroad tracks dimly lit by the stars and the shrinking moon.

I stuck to the tracks and ran like a hunted deer. The tracks led me farther and farther from the police lights on the highway. I didn't think I was being followed, but I kept looking back to make sure. I stumbled a few extra miles before I pulled up, gasping for air. My lungs were on fire. My side hurt like I had a sword in it.

I could barely believe what had happened back there. What if I'd been deported to Guatemala? What then?

What now? I didn't even have the money for a bus ticket home. Not that I would be safe on a bus. Crazy, that I needed documents in my own country. My mother hadn't thought of that. The only documents we had spoken of were the fake ones I would need to buy in the States—fake Social Security, fake green card. I could only guess that my father had never mentioned having to show documents in Mexico.

A bolt of fear ran through me on the railroad tracks. It left me shivering despite my jacket and the heat of running. I was in bad trouble. From out of nowhere, one of my father's proverbs came to mind: "It's a bad start on the week for the man who is hanged on a Monday."

I laughed a crazy, desperate laugh. This helped, hearing my father's voice, seeing the twinkle in his eyes. I had to get hold of myself. What direction had I been running on the tracks—north or south?

I remembered that I knew how to find the North Star. When my father was back from his first year on the other side, I had asked him where El Norte was. "Under that star," he replied, and showed me how to find it.

I found it now, and discovered that I had been running north. At least I'd been going in the direction of the border.

I thought about turning around, trying to make my way home. But what then? What was the family going to do then?

There was no turning back, nothing to do but keep walking. "Better to die on your feet than lie on your knees," I heard Papá saying.

As I walked on, the lights of a town in the distance were slow to get any closer. The moon set, and I walked by the starlight. I kept going, eyelids heavy as metal. After a while I noticed wearily that I was casting a long shadow. I didn't stop to wonder why, with dawn still hours away. Like a rabbit that doesn't hear the approach of the swooping eagle, I had no idea what was bearing down on me.

When at last I spun around, I was blinded by an oncoming eye bright as the sun. A terrible blast sounded, once, twice, three times, and I ran stumbling off the tracks. I fell back onto my elbows, and shuddered at a freight train hurtling through the darkness. My fright turned to amazement as I made out the silhouettes of riders clinging to the iron monster.

Before long I was walking the tracks again, wondering about those riders and recalling their backpacks. They were on their way to the border. What a dangerous way to go!

Either those people couldn't afford the bus, or they couldn't risk it. It was easy enough to guess that they were illegal in Mexico, and this was how they were sneaking through. It hit me hard, what this meant. This is the way I was going to have to travel now, like an outlaw in my own country.

Dawn came and went as I put one foot in front of the other. Finally I reached the town. It was too small even to have a sign announcing its name. Another freight train rumbled through without stopping. This one also had riders with backpacks.

With only my mother's last tamales for fuel, I walked all day. I got many chances to watch riders as they flew by on the northbound freights. Finally the tracks led to a bigger town, where the trains would stop, or so I hoped. I left the tracks and approached the depot from the street. Acaponeta, the sign said.

A train pulled in, and it stopped for a few minutes, but it was a passenger train and useless to me. When dark came, I hid in the train yards, around the corner of a warehouse. A guard was on duty but he wasn't paying any attention. Two freight trains roared on through. Soon, I was going to have to keep going on foot.

It must have been around midnight when a freight rolled clanking and hissing into the yards. As it slowed, I got ready to dash under the yard lights. The train had riders, lots of them—men, women, teenagers. Mostly they were bunched at the backs of the rounded fuel cars, where a narrow platform with a handrail made a perfect place for standing and hanging on. Some people clung to the rungs of the ladders that ran up the outside of the boxcars. All but a few of these had tied themselves to the rungs with the arms of a shirt passed behind their waist. Quickly, I got my long-sleeve shirt out of my bag and tied it around mine just in case.

Instead of grinding to a halt, the train started to pick up speed. It wasn't stopping after all. The last few cars were still in reach. I slung my bag over my shoulder and took off running.

The light was poor. I had my eye on the ladder toward the back of an approaching boxcar. I was running full out alongside, fast as my legs could go. If I tripped, or if I slipped, I would fall under the wheels. The moment of truth arrived. I timed my leap and grabbed hold of a rung with both hands. I swung my feet up and reached for a higher rung, pulling, kicking, and scratching until my feet found the bottom rung. I was standing on the ladder.

My chest was heaving, as much with fright as anything. I hadn't realized how difficult it was going to be. I'd never done anything so dangerous, not nearly.

Before long the train was up to full speed. It rocked and swayed, enough to throw me off if I loosened my grip even for a second. The miles went by, and so did the time. I hadn't slept since leaving home. I began to imagine I was lying in my bed. Stop that, I told myself. Relax, and you will die. I was so exhausted I had forgotten about the shirt tied around my waist, and what it was for. Remembering, I managed to tie myself to the ladder.

Whether the shirt would hold me, I didn't want to find out. I fought the weariness by imagining I was already in El Norte, working in the fields, sending the first money home to my mother. I had many conversations in my mind. Some of them were with my family, but mostly they were with Rico. When I told him I had jumped onto a moving train, he laughed at me. He didn't believe it. He said I was making it up. "Turtle, you would never do a thing like that, not in a million years."

By now Rico and the four men from the village had met their coyote. They had already given over the big money and were crossing the wire. At this very minute, Rico was walking across the desert. Before long, he would be in the swimming pool at his brother's house in Tucson.

I don't know how much time had gone by. It was the middle of the night when I was startled awake. The train was slowing. I had fallen asleep standing up. And now someone was yelling at me, someone from on top of the boxcar. I looked up and saw the silhouette of a head and elbows. "Hey, you," the man yelled. "Heads up!"

"What's going on?" I called back.

"Police, and lots of them."

I looked around. The train was pulling into the yards. What city this was, I had no idea. "I don't see any police!" I said.

"They're hiding, what do you think?"

"How do you know?"

"That's the word from the front. Get ready to jump, fool. I'm coming down right behind you."

Suddenly, the whistle blasted twice. Growling and hissing, the iron beast was braking some more. I looked ahead along the track and saw police and soldiers lurking in the shadows. The man was right. I was going to have to jump off.

When, that was the question. The ground was flying by. The train was still going too fast.

"Get ready!" yelled the man from above. He was starting down the ladder.

Forget him. I wasn't going to jump until I saw other people jumping.

I leaned away from the boxcar to get a better look ahead and discovered I was tied on. Suddenly I was boiling in panic. I managed to undo the knot. The shirt dropped and disappeared under the wheels of the train.

47

"Move it!" yelled the man from above. His feet were on the rung just above my hands.

"Shut up!" I hollered back. It was all a blur—train wheels spinning, voices shouting, the ground speeding below, the shadowy shapes of riders up ahead beginning to jump from the train, police running out to grab them.

"Jump! Jump now!" the man above screamed, and I did. I tried to run in the air, knowing I had to tumble away from the wheels as I landed, but the train yard was too dark and everything was moving too fast. The ground seemed to fly up. It hit me hard, and I blacked out.

8

Julio

THE SIREN OF THE AMBULANCE was the next thing I heard. High on the side of my head, it felt like my scalp had been opened up with a shovel. In the hospital, they shaved around the wound, cleaned it, and stitched it up. I had never been in a hospital before, never had stitches before. I was frightened as a baby rabbit at the bottom of a bucket. I was too afraid to answer the doctor's questions.

The doctor said it would take me awhile to get my memory back, but he was wrong about that. I hadn't lost my memory, and I knew why a policeman was keeping an eye on me from the door. The doctor said they were going to hold me at the hospital until it was safe for me to travel. I sneaked out three hours later, when the policeman stepped away to get something to eat or visit the bathroom. Fortunately, I still had my shoulder bag, even my crumpled straw hat.

I spent the day where it felt safest, in Mazatlán's most crowded streets. Over and over, I wondered if I should just give up and try to go back home. But that wouldn't solve anything. Somehow, I had to get to El Norte. Late in the day I headed for the train yards. There was no way around it: I had to get back on a train. This time I had to be smarter, and hope for better luck.

In and around the yards, there were many places to hide, and many people hiding. At dusk, a train showed signs of pulling out at any second. Everyone ran, like a flock of birds bursting from the trees and flying to the same fence wire. By the grace of God, the security guards stood by and watched the stampede without even letting on that they noticed.

I was about to join the many people running for the empty flat-cars, but I was wary of joining them. Wouldn't they be the first to get kicked off? Just then a boy at my elbow veered off toward some flatcars stacked with automobile carriers. I sprinted to catch up, then panted, "Mind if I come with you?"

"Why not?" he called as we ran. He had a wide, friendly smile and wild hair that stood straight up. He was my size, my age, with the same dark brown skin. I watched as he climbed onto a coupling and jumped down onto the ground on the other side. I did the same. The train lurched into motion. "Hurry!" he yelled over his shoulder. "I know a trick!"

I ran to catch up, afraid I'd lost my chance to catch this train. Loping along in the shadow of one of the towering, enclosed automobile carriers, the boy sized it up as if picking out a horse. The vehicles, three across and three high, showed through narrow gaps in the metal siding. The metal doors at the ends of the carrier were locked shut.

The wild-haired boy sprang for a ladder and climbed. I hated the idea of hanging on to another ladder for miles on end, but now I had no choice, not if I was going to catch this train. Too late now to do anything but leap and grab and climb up after him.

As I climbed, the train picked up speed. Three mojados were running alongside, still hoping to get on board, but the train was already moving too fast. Disappointment was written large on their faces.

With all the racket and motion, my stomach churned and my head swam. I had nothing to tie myself on with. What was to keep me from falling?

"Keep coming, amigo," called the voice from above, so full of confidence. He scampered the rest of the way up the ladder, then disappeared over the top. What in the world?

High on the ladder, high as an eagle's nest, I looked over the roof. My wild companion was nowhere to be seen.

"Drop your bag first," called his echoing voice.

Holding for dear life to the top of the ladder, I leaned over a narrow opening. It wasn't so far to the floor—an easy drop if the train was standing still. To get inside, I was going to have to climb on top of the train first, and it was swaying like a tree in a windstorm. I looked away for a second, and that was a mistake. The ground was a long, long way down, and everything was a blur. My legs began to tremble. "You can do it!" called that encouraging voice.

I don't have any choice, I thought. I threw my bag inside, then climbed onto the roof of the carrier. For a second, I thought the wind would blow me off, but I kept my balance and got down fast. My hands held, my legs cooperated, and I dropped to safety in front of a brand-new Suburban.

"Easy as can be!" cried the boy, whose bright smile was gleaming in the darkness. So were the brand-new Suburbans as they caught some light from above and from slits in the metal walls. "How do you like it? Pretty good, no?"

"How come no police today, no soldiers?"

"Sometimes it's hot and sometimes it's not."

"How far can we take this train?"

"All the way to Nogales, I'm pretty sure. These cars are heading to Phoenix, that's what I heard. Hey, there's some blood showing through your hat. Are you bleeding?"

"Maybe," I said. I took my hat off carefully.

"Bleeding, but not that bad," he reported. "Got some stitches under there, I bet. Radical look, how it's shaved all around the bandage. How do you like mine?"

"Your what?"

"My haircut!"

I took another look. I remembered an animal I had seen in a book. "It's wild," I said. "Sticks up like porcupine quills."

His smile vanished. "Like when a porcupine is afraid? My head looks like the rear end of a frightened porcupine, is that what you're saying?"

"Kind of . . . I mean, it looks really good."

He started laughing. "I like that, Stitches. That's a good one. How did you get hurt?"

"Jumped off a train last night—lots of police and soldiers."

"I was on the same train. You jumped too soon. You weren't the only one to get hurt. Did you hear about the woman from El Salvador?"

"No, nothing."

"They say she was on her way to New York City to work in a restaurant. She lost both her legs, but was still alive when they took her away. I heard she has three small children back home. It could have happened to you. You must be new at this."

"First time."

"It's simple. Don't try to get on or off if the train is moving faster than you can run. Last year I saw a man get killed in four pieces. A couple of weeks ago, some Maras threw me off, and the train was going way too fast. I got lucky. I bounced like a rubber ball."

"Who are Maras?"

"Where are you from, anyway?"

I hesitated. "Chiapas," I said.

"No way."

"Why not?"

"If you were from Chiapas, you'd know what Maras are."

"So, what are they?"

"Tell me first, where are you really from?"

"Near Silao, where they put together these Suburbans."

"So how come you said you were from Chiapas?"

"Because when I say I'm from Guanajuato, nobody believes me."

"I would have, if you gave me a chance."

"I was born in Chiapas."

"So, you're Mexican, that's what you're telling me."

"No identification, that's the problem. I feel like the whole Mexican army is after me. They seem to think I'm from Guatemala."

"I'm Julio," the boy said, and stuck out his hand. "Julio from Honduras, a small village outside of San Pedro Sula."

"Victor," I said as I offered mine. "Victor from Mexico, a small village outside Silao."

"Don't lie to me again, 'mano—okay?"

"Promise."

"You're not very good at it. You're the worst liar I ever met."

"So, what are those Maras you were talking about?"

"The biggest and worst gang there is, if you're from Guatemala or Chiapas. They've taken over the railroads. They rob everybody who's trying to get across the border into Mexico. You got any money?"

"Eighty centavos."

"I picked a rich one. How do you expect to get across the wire without coyote money?"

"I don't know, to tell you the truth. Do all these people on these freight trains have coyote money?"

"Almost all of them. You have to be really crazy, really stupid, or really poor to cross the border without a coyote."

"What about you?"

"I'm all three. It's going to be a long ride, Victor. Let's make ourselves comfortable."

Julio said we were going to search for keys to the Suburbans — they must be hidden somewhere. It was too much trouble for the factory to send the keys separately to El Norte. "My best friend's brother-in-law works at the plant in Silao," I said.

"So?"

"He just does."

"Weren't you about to say that he told you where they hide the keys?"

"Nothing that helpful."

"They might be anywhere," Julio said as he slid under the first car. I went to my knees and started searching the next one. It was like trying to milk a goat in the pitch dark. After searching behind the grill, the license plates, and the underside of the engine, I felt a bump on the side of the frame near the back, under a smooth strip of tape. A minute later, we were inside the vehicle, enjoying the comfortable, plastic-covered seats.

Julio, in the driver's seat, turned the electricity on but not the motor. He turned the radio on and started punching through the channels. "What kind of music you like?"

"Anything — ranchera, mostly."

"I like ranchera." He kept punching until he found that loud, clear signal from Radio XEG in Monterrey. "There, we have music. Everything is lively and good. You got any food, got any water?"

"Got water."

"I don't believe you. You think you're going to just fly across the border like a bird or a bat? What is your plan?"

"Every man is entitled to make a kite out of his pants."

"That's a good one! Where'd you get that?"

"From my father—he's dead."

"Well, mine isn't, but sometimes maybe he wishes he was. You can't eat if you can't work."

Julio must have found a hidden switch. Suddenly his seat went way back, almost like a bed. He laughed and pretended he was snoring, then grew quiet as he drifted off. For the time being, getting to know each other was over.

I figured out how to make my own seat go back and fell asleep despite my hunger, the pounding of my wound, and the fact that I had to pee.

I woke to the sound of the car door opening. Julio climbed out and stood over a crack in the floor. I could hear his stream splashing on the car below. I started laughing, and he did, too. He said to cut it out, he couldn't concentrate. He got back in and I left to do the same. When I got back I asked him what to do about the other kind. He said not to even think about it.

"How did you know about getting inside here?" I asked him.

"A guy told me."

"Ever done it before?"

"Never."

"Been to the States before?"

"Last year, but it wasn't easy. I would've crossed into California—San Diego—but I heard they built a big metal wall all across there. I decided to try to find my aunt and uncle instead, in Texas."

"Was it easy to cross into Texas?"

"Are you kidding? It took me eight tries."

"What is it really like in the States?"

"You'll have to see for yourself. It's impossible to explain. It's so different, it's like another world."

"Is it good? Is it bad?"

"It's both."

Julio didn't like to talk about it, same as my father. "Papá," I once asked my father, "why is El Norte so rich?" He only smiled and made a joke: "God gives money to the wealthy because without it, they would starve to death."

I got back to the subject of crossing. "Julio, why are you trying to cross into Arizona this time?"

"Because everybody is saying Arizona is the way to go. Its border is so long, so full of deserts and mountains, the Migra are like a hundred cats trying to catch a million mice. You know about La Migra, I take it."

"American immigration, U.S. Border Patrol. That much I do know. What kind of work will you try to do this time?"

"Anything. I'll wash dishes in a restaurant, sack groceries, do landscaping or construction. I'll even pick lettuce. I'm a good worker, and they're always looking for good workers up there. The truth is, they know we work harder than they do. Grab my backpack off the backseat, will you? I'm busy driving."

"What do you need?"

"Food and water. You hungry?"

9

Nogales

I HAD NEVER UNDERSTOOD before, what a long, long way it was to the border. The train continued on through the night and into the next morning and afternoon. Whenever it stopped, we knew we were in danger. We would turn the radio off and listen to the sounds from outside. Once, we heard people running, and the shouts of police ordering them to stop. I was sure that our hiding place would be searched, but it wasn't. After half an hour, the train was moving again.

Inside our Suburban, there was hardly any rocking motion and practically no noise. I rested easy again. Julio was pretty sure that the carrier wouldn't be searched until the final inspection before the crossing of the border, when every nook and cranny of these vehicles would be searched for people and drugs.

I asked how we would know when it was time to get out, and Julio said we would wait until a stop lasted for an hour. Until then, we wouldn't even poke our heads out to see where we were.

"How will you know it is Nogales?"

"Because I've been told what it looks like. It's a city spread all over the hills, looking down into Nogales, Arizona, which they say is much smaller. There's a metal fence, more like a wall, in between."

"How is that possible to be looking down from Mexico into the States? Aren't they above us?"

"Listen, I'm telling you what I heard. Here's something else. There are two really long tunnels that run under the border. They carry the storm waters that run off the Mexican hills. That's how I'm going to cross. You can come with me if you want."

"Wouldn't you drown?"

"The tunnels are dry most of the time. People live in them, that's what I heard. Street kids. Cholos."

"Gangs?"

"They take people through for money, but if you know the password, they'll just let you go by."

"Do you know the password?"

"Forward and backward."

"What about the police on the Mexican side and the Border Patrol on the American side? Don't they try to stop people from crossing through the tunnels? It sounds too good to be true!"

"Have you been living under a stone? On the Mexican side, the police are easily bribed."

"Who bribes them?"

"The coyotes, who else? In this case, it would be the cholos. As for the American side, who knows? Maybe the Border Patrol doesn't watch their end of the tunnels all the time. Maybe they get paid off, too."

"It sounds like you have it all figured out."

"You never have it all figured out. Something unexpected always happens. You do what you can and hope for good luck."

"Did you have good luck once you finally got to your aunt and uncle's in Texas?"

"At first I did. I worked five months at a turkey farm."

"Doing what?"

"Sweeping, mopping, shoveling, chopping heads, plucking feathers, pulling the guts out. Hard work, 'mano, but I was good at it. I was able to make good money and send hundreds of dollars home to my parents, for them and my brothers and sisters. But then the police came. My aunt and my uncle were always fighting. The neighbors got tired of it."

"Did you get to keep your job?"

"Are you kidding? They went to jail, and so did I. We were all illegal. If you stay out of trouble up there, they'll leave you alone. They need the workers. But if you get into trouble, your life is like a tin can that gets kicked down the road."

"They deported you back to Honduras?"

"Eventually, on an airplane, with a Migra escort just for me if you can believe it. What a view. I was flying like a bird, above the clouds sometimes. Even when you are below the clouds, you're still so high that the cars and houses look tiny."

"I can only imagine! What did you mean, they deported you 'eventually'?"

"They kept me in jail four months."

"Really?"

"Really. Two months in the juvenile detention, but then it got so crowded, I had to wait in the county jail. Why it took so long, I have no idea. That jail was a scary place, 'mano. Tejanos, Mexicans, Central Americans, blacks, Anglos . . . it was like five different animals dropped into a barrel."

"Anglos? I thought all the gabachos were rich. What were they doing in jail?"

"You don't know very much about El Norte."

"What were the guards like?"

"They were mean. They liked to throw the lights on in the middle of the night, get you out of bed, search your cell while a vicious dog growled and snapped at you. They let the dog come within this close of biting you, and then they pull him back."

"So, here you are heading north again."

"What else? You never go hungry there, once you find work. When I told my father I was going to go back to El Norte, he said, 'If you want to go, go.' In Honduras, on days he can find work, all he makes is a dollar and a half American, and that's doing construction. Sometimes, when I could get away with it, I could make two dollars, stealing bananas from the company plantation and selling them in San Pedro Sula. If you're a kid from the village, forget about a real job."

"How much did you make in El Norte?"

"Six dollars an hour, ten hours a day."

"Sixty American dollars in a day? Is that possible?"

"Believe it. That's why I'm going back."

"What did your mother say?"

"She said, 'Okay, go try. God bless you.' I found a seashell yesterday that I'm going to give her eventually. Who knows when."

"In between trains, you traveled to the ocean?"

"Guess what? Mazatlán is on the ocean."

"I didn't know it was that close. I always wanted to see the ocean. I missed my chance!"

It was dark, early evening, when we finally climbed out through the roof of the automobile carrier. Julio was sure we had reached Nogales. We were able to sneak through the train yards, past warehouses and abandoned boxcars with families living inside. A little girl had her hand out begging. We soon reached the lights of the city, with the border wall in sight. The traffic was all backed up.

"They're waiting to get through the Port of Entry gates," Julio said. "C'mon, let's take a look around."

I don't know what I would have done if I hadn't been with Julio. He had never been in Nogales either, but from the way he carried himself, you would never believe it.

The air smelled of broiling meat and onions from the taco carts, and of diesel fumes. That much was like Silao, but there were many more gabachos. Fresh from the States, they were flocking to the shops down the street. Taxis were honking at kids racing through the traffic to beg work from Mexicans returning from the American Nogales, arms full of shopping bags. Julio explained that some people had the documents to cross back and forth.

With me at his elbow, Julio threaded his way through the crowds and the tourist shops, the pharmacies, past some hotels with campesinos spilling out of the lobbies onto the streets. I told him that in Silao, farmers never stayed in hotels.

"Before they stitched up your head, Victor, did some of your brains spill out? Those are mojados. They haven't crossed the border yet, but can't you see how wet they are? The ones lined up at those pay phones over there are talking with relatives and labor contractors on the other side. See that one with the straw hat over there, talking to the slick guy? That's a leader of a mojado group bargaining with a coyote. Getting the bad news about how much it's going to cost."

Ahead, people were milling around an ice-cream cart. A girl bought a chocolate-covered frozen banana on a stick. My eyes followed it to her mouth. All I'd eaten since my mother's tamales was a can of stew Julio had shared with me on the train. I closed my eyes and imagined the taste of the chocolate-covered frozen banana. My stomach felt like a small animal with claws, but that was nothing new.

We kept moving. We walked along a narrow, cobbled street lined with homes, mostly of concrete. Every window was barred with heavy wrought iron. The yard walls were high and studded with broken glass. The border rap thumping from car speakers set me on edge and so did the number of police, all different kinds. Nogales wasn't anything like Silao. How were we even going to find a safe place to sleep?

We walked around the Plaza de Toros, our eyes on the bullfighting murals. The entrance of the arena was swarming with street kids. We came to a small park wedged between streets with heavy traffic, where kids darted out to wash windshields at the stoplights. In the center of the park, taquerías and other carts ringed the bronze statue of a man whose head was a bathroom for pigeons.

Not far away, we looked over a guardrail into the yawning opening of a huge concrete storm tunnel. "Look, we've already found one," Julio said. About seven feet high and twice as wide, the tunnel drained a dry wash that ran down from the hills. All around the mouth of the tunnel, the concrete was spray-painted with graffiti: names, slogans that cursed the police, symbols I couldn't read, and the words Los Vampiros.

The entrance was poorly lit, but we could see kids hanging around outside and others disappearing inside. One of the kids, sitting in the shadows on a broken slab of concrete, held a paper bag to his face, like a horse with its muzzle in a feed bag. "What in the world is he doing?" I asked Julio.

"You really don't know? He sprayed paint in there, and now he's inhaling the fumes. His brains are cheese!"

We turned away from the city center. Narrow lanes led up the gullies and into a neighborhood on the hillside where dogs barked and the headlights of cars fell on kids kicking balls in a rain of dust. Some of the houses were made of concrete blocks or adobe bricks, and looked like my family home. Others were stitched together of boards, plywood, tar paper, mud, and cardboard, with roofs of metal sheeting weighted by tires, rocks, even wheelbarrows. A strong windstorm might blow them down. A heavy rain, and they might slide into the gullies.

Below the hills, the tall metal border wall, topped with barbed wire, was bathed in stadium lights from one end of the city to the other. On the American side, a strip of bare ground was patrolled by green-and-white trucks that Julio said were the Border Patrol. Kids were throwing rocks from our side of the wall down onto the American side, trying to hit one of the Migra trucks.

We kept climbing in search of a place to hide and sleep. We followed the edge of a landslide full of garbage. At last we found a patch of hillside without houses. A lone mesquite tree drew us like a magnet.

Julio called as we got close. No one answered. We crawled under the sheltering branches. There was garbage strewn around, some spray cans, the smell of urine, but no one was there. We spread out our blankets, put our heads down, and hoped for the best.

10

Keeping Our Eyes Open

T

HE CHOLOS CAME IN THE middle of the night. I was in a deep sleep, and so was Julio. They woke us with kicks. There were six of them, two with flashlights. They said it was their tree. The girl who was with them giggled when they said we owed them rent. She went through our things.

"We'll just leave," Julio said.

"Not until you pay," growled their leader, the biggest of the pack. He was wearing baggy clothes and gleaming white sneakers.

"No money," reported the girl. "Nothing in their stuff worth anything." Like the others, she had a triangle of blue dots tattooed on her wrist. All had weird-looking rings of fresh gold paint around their mouths.

The boys moved in closer, like wolves to the kill. The youngest one, no older than ten, was keeping a powerful flashlight beam in my eyes. I pulled the coins out my jeans pocket and told them it was all that I had. An unseen hand struck my wrist, and the coins went flying.

"Hey, you guys," Julio said in a friendly voice. "Paisano twenty-seven."

"What's that supposed to mean?" cackled the leader. He had a voice like a crow.

"It means you let us go," Julio said.

They all started laughing. Their leader said, "That's the same stupid so-called password we keep hearing in Los Vampiros. You chuntaros, there's no password. It is only a joke going around to be played on lowlifes like you from Honduras or Guatemala or wherever you're from. Now give us your money, the serious money."

I didn't mind being called a stupid, skinny fool. Chuntaro described how I felt to find myself completely at their mercy. Meanwhile, Julio's face hardened. Suddenly he looked tough and dangerous, nothing like the boy I had known on the train.

"Your money," croaked the crow.

"Try his pants," giggled the girl.

The pack moved closer yet. "I'll get it myself," Julio growled. A flashlight beam followed his hand as it slid under his belt. Next thing I saw was a blunt piece of metal, out of which jumped a deadly looking blade. "Who wants it?" Julio roared, and they all jumped back. He started waving the knife wildly, lunging at the cholos. They ran like rats dumped out of a sack, and they didn't come back.

"I don't believe you," I cried, half in admiration and half in shock. "They could've killed us. What if they also had weapons?"

"They would have had to use them."

"You had big money after all? Coyote money?"

"I got nothing, same as you."

"Then, why—"

"I was keeping my pants on, that's all. Let's get out of here."

"Maybe I can find my coins."

"Those paintheads might come back. Grab your things and let's go."

We stumbled across the hillside in the eerie glow from the light towers along the border. Chuntaro, I told myself. How are you going to get across now?

We made our way downtown, to the bus terminal. In the middle of the night, it was full of people who looked half dead. Eventually, a bench opened up. As soon as we sat down, we were joined by a slouching man with a large silver belt buckle. "Where are you going?" he asked as he lit a cigarette. His face was flushed and he smelled of liquor.

"Don't know," Julio said, "and we don't have any money to get there."

"Aaah," the man replied. "You have nothing. Nothing but nothing."

The man took a long pull on his cigarette, slowly let it out. "There's money to be made in the desert . . . if you have strong backs."

"And if we get caught," Julio replied, "we go to jail for ten years, maybe twenty or thirty, no?"

"What is the matter with you two? You have to think positive, or you'll never get anywhere in life."

"Thank you for your advice, señor," Julio said respectfully. "We will consider what you had to say."

"I'll be around," he said, and shambled away.

"Drugs?" I asked, when the recruiter had vanished.

"What else? They always need mules to replace the ones that get caught."

"Are you actually going to consider it, like you said? And risk jail?"

"Do I look like I had a horse for a mother and a jackass for a father? Did you forget that I've already been in prison? Did I make it sound like a holiday in Cancún?"

"Sorry if I've irritated you, Julio."

"You haven't, 'mano. Nogales has. I don't want to spend a minute longer at the bottom of this outhouse than I have to."

"I'm with you," I said.

He laughed bitterly. "The password is no good, but there's always another way. We just have to keep our eyes open."

Daytime found us looking for work at the gas stations, the small groceries, the tourist shops, tire repairs, shoe repairs, and a small factory that made roof tiles. People shook us off. They didn't even want to talk.

At the Port of Entry, we tried to make a little money carrying shopping bags for people returning from the other side, mostly from the Wal-Mart. I recognized the blue bags from the Wal-Mart in Silao. The problem was, there were too many kids. It was like a flock of sparrows going for the same few seeds. We didn't have any luck. My hunger felt like a clenched fist.

At a taquería, Julio bought tacos for both of us. We sat on a low wall close by and ate very slowly. Julio was watching a young man trying to buy something to eat. He had the chest of a bull and arms like tree trunks. I started paying attention and noticed that he could barely speak Spanish. He looked as Mexican as anybody, yet it was all he could do to order two tacos. He had an American ten dollar bill in his hand.

"Ten," the vendor said. The young man looked very confused as he handed over the bill.

The vendor hadn't missed the confusion. In fact, he took advantage of it. He put the ten dollars away quickly and started helping the next person. The young man stood there for a second with his tacos. Then he turned away, looking lost as a bird that's just hit a window. For some reason, he didn't understand Mexican money. He had just paid more than ten times too much.

Julio jumped up and got in the middle of it. With some weak excuse I couldn't hear, the vendor had to hand over the change. The young man with the muscles gave half to Julio as a gift, then sat beside us on the wall and started in on his tacos.

Julio spoke enough English to have a conversation with him. I didn't understand a word except his name, Hector. Later, as we went our separate ways, Julio told me that Hector was from

Colorado. He'd been deported only the day before. Hector hadn't been in Mexico for nineteen years, ever since crossing on his mother's back. He grew up American, but without documents. He graduated from high school and was a football star—American football. He had a good job at a place that sold farm machinery. A week ago, he'd had a little traffic accident. When he couldn't show the police a driver's license, even a fake one, they took him in and then the Border Patrol got ahold of him.

"Can you believe it?" Julio said.

"What's he going to do?"

"Pay the coyotes to take him across."

"The cholos, through one of the tunnels?"

"He told me he'd almost been tricked into trying that. Just in time, he found out that the Americans had recently closed the tunnels on their side with chain-link gates. They only open them up when it's flooding—so the cholos who live inside won't get pinned against them and drown. You know what, Victor? Before it gets dark, we better find out where it's safe to sleep."

Our search ended at the Plaza de Toros, which turned out no longer to be a bullfighting arena. The city had turned it into a place for the homeless to sleep. We went inside to take a look. The protected places under the colonnades were already marked off by families and were filled with their belongings, with kids keeping guard. No matter—there was no sign of rain. We spread out our blankets in the middle of the arena.

Julio was in a bad mood the next day, and I knew why. He had been counting on the tunnels. I asked him what he thought about hiking east or west along the border, then crossing someplace past where the metal wall ended.

"I'm afraid it might come to that," Julio said darkly. "From what I hear, it's a long, long way across the desert—four, five days, maybe a week. Without a coyote to guide us, what would be our chances?"

"If the tunnel wasn't closed, and the password had worked, what were you going to do once you got to the other side?"

"Get back on the train. On the way to Phoenix, it goes through Tucson. From what I hear, those are cities where we would blend right in."

"Tucson is where my friend was going—to his brother's house— but he had coyote money."

"There has to be a way, if we just keep our eyes open. Meanwhile, we need to figure out how to feed our stomachs."

11

Frozen in Place

W E WENT LOOKING FOR WORK again, but came up empty. We had just passed by a church when I happened to glance through the open door of the next building. Inside, people were eating at rows upon rows of long tables. We took a look. It didn't seem like anyone was taking money. We asked a woman with small children who was on her way out what was going on. "This is the church's soup kitchen," she said. "They're open every day for comida. Hurry in, they'll stop serving soon."

Rice and beans with bits of meat along with two tortillas sure felt good in my stomach. "I take back what I said about Nogales," Julio said.

Afterward we were walking by the small park between busy streets, the one with the man of bronze that the pigeons liked so much. The Stupid Dummy, kids called the statue, the kids who ran into the street at the stoplight to sell gum and wash windshields.

"Want to try that?" I asked Julio. "Buy some gum and resell it?"

He answered with a sour expression. Just then a kid tossed a squeeze bottle and a rag behind a taco cart. I grabbed them up. "It's worth a try," I said.

"Go ahead," Julio said. "I'll see you tonight at the Plaza de Toros."

The kids washing windshields were only eight, nine, ten years old. They yelled at me, but only at first. This was no way to get rich. The drivers mostly wagged their fingers at me. Others ignored me, let me wash their windshield, and drove off. Every so often, someone gave a little. An American gave me a dollar bill. By the end of the day I had enough to buy extra food for a couple of days, but I was going to try not to spend it.

That night at the Plaza de Toros, Julio showed up with his backpack in his hand and a new one on his back. The new one was heavy with food—bags of tortillas, blocks of cheese, cans of meat and chili peppers and so on. He spread them out on the blanket for me to look at. "For crossing the desert?" I asked.

"Possibly," he said. He opened up a package of tortillas, handed me a few, took a few for himself. Out came his knife. Julio popped the stiletto blade and carved some hunks off the cheese. With his can opener, he opened a can of peppers. "Dig in," he said.

I did as I was told. "I was hungry," I said.

"That's what I thought."

It was then I realized he must have stolen the pack, probably from a fellow mojado, maybe at the bus terminal, somewhere like that. "Let's split the food—it's heavy," Julio said. "You keep the pack. It's more useful than that bag of yours."

I already knew I wasn't going to ask him any hard questions. "Thanks," I said.

We were going to keep eating at the church's soup kitchen. We would save the rest of the canned goods, in case we needed to cross the desert on foot.

The days passed with me making only pocket money and Julio away on his own business, which I never asked about. March was melting away. I was keeping track of the days in my head. It might be seven months before the Day of the Dead, when my family would have to move away if I failed to send money from El Norte, but that didn't mean I had time to spare. Crossing the desert in summer would be too dangerous. If I could cross soon and send money home before summer, they wouldn't have to sell our milk goat. They could keep her and her kids, due in the middle of April. Usually she had two. My family would have milk and cheese and meat to go with the garden vegetables.

The fourth day in Nogales, heavy clouds rolled in. My skin was no longer so dry, and neither was my throat. The air, full of moisture, even smelled different.

Still, I didn't guess the weather would come to anything, and neither did Julio. We spread out our blankets as usual that night, along with the others in the center of the bullfighting arena. Sometime after midnight, the clouds broke open with bolts of lightning, booming thunder, and sheets of rain. We ran for cover and squeezed into a tiny space under the colonnades.

The lightning kept cracking and the thunder rumbling. There were many crying babies and not much sleep. Dawn came, and it was still spitting rain. Julio was all excited and wanted to go outside, into the streets. I grabbed my new backpack and ran after him.

Julio made like an arrow to the mouth of Los Vampiros, the tunnel close to the city center. The wash that came down from the hills and into the tunnel was running fast and deep. The floodwater was black with muck and heaving with sticks, plastic jugs, odds and ends of garbage. "This is our ticket to El Norte!" Julio cried, and started running the opposite direction.

"What are you talking about?" I yelled as I ran to keep up.

"Just stick with me. You'll see!"

At the nearest gas station, Julio pulled out a roll of pesos and bought two large inner tubes. "You mean to float through?" I cried.

"What else?" He soon had them inflated, and we were running back toward Los Vampiros. My heart was in my throat. "I don't know," I summoned the courage to tell him. "I just don't know."

Julio ignored me, just kept running. At a nearby store, he darted inside and bought two flashlights, one of which he shoved into my hand. "They say it's almost two miles long, and pitch dark."

"I don't know, that sounds really risky," I murmured, with only a block to go. All I could think of was how lucky I had been to survive my leap from the train. This was going to be an even bigger leap.

We got to the guardrail above the raging arroyo. Julio climbed over the rail and started to make his way down the other side. Cautiously, I followed him down. I glanced over my shoulder. A couple of cholos were up above, standing at the guardrail. I couldn't tell a thing from their expressions, whether they thought this was going to work or we were going to die.

Julio set his inner tube down at the edge of the black, muddy river and then took his pack off his back. I just stood there like the Stupid Dummy statue. "Are you coming, or not?" he said, wild-eyed.

"Julio, what if they didn't open the gates at the other end?"

"I'm going to take that chance! An opportunity like this, with the cholos out of the way and the Border Patrol off guard . . . don't you see? Don't you see?"

"Maybe so . . . If it was just me, I would do it."

"What are you talking about?" he yelled.

"What if the gate is closed? What if I drown? What would happen to my family? I can't take the chance. I'll have to find another way."

Julio threw up his hands. "Good-bye, then, amigo. Good luck to you!" He waded into the water, settled into the inner tube with his backpack to his chest, and pushed off, flashlight in hand.

In seconds, without a look back, he disappeared into the blackness.

It wasn't long before the river quit running through the tunnel. The water remaining was only ankle deep. Dozens of cholos went back into the tunnel to reclaim what was left of their empire. I asked one about the gate at the other end, if he thought it had been opened in time. "How would I know?" he said. "I ran out of this end, can't you tell?"

I found the answer the next day, in the newspaper. The gates had been opened. Nobody had drowned. It didn't say a thing about people running or floating out of the other end. It just didn't say. But I had a picture in my mind. Julio had floated all the way through, and right past the Border Patrol. I could picture the patrolmen running along the bank, trying to catch up with him.

I pictured Julio landing his inner tube and running for it. I could see him back on the train, safe inside a Suburban heading for Tucson and Phoenix.

I would never know. I would only know I had been too cautious, just like Rico had always said.

I could see Rico's grin. I could hear him calling me Turtle.

In a daze, I went back to work washing windshields at the Stupid Dummy stoplight. "What is the matter with you?" asked a kid Chuy's age. "Are you stupid?"

"What are you talking about?" I fired back.

"You're old enough to get a job at one of the maquiladoras. My mother makes five dollars a day."

"Doing what?"

"Putting TVs together."

"Do they need people?"

"What do you think? There's a hundred of those factories. That's where everybody works. You just have to be old enough."

"Where are they?"

The boy pointed. "Over the hills, everywhere you look."

"I'll give it a try," I said. "Many thanks."

"It's nothing," he said, and raced into the traffic with his squeeze bottle.

I hiked through the neighborhoods and over the hills, where dirt roads led to the assembly plants. They were big as bus terminals and enclosed by chain link fences. Before I reached the gate of the nearest factory, the man at the guardhouse motioned for me to go away. I hiked to the next one. This one had little traffic, and the guard was willing to speak to me. "This plant is closed," he said. "It's been closed since January."

"Where should I go? Which one would have work?"

"None of them. A dozen have closed already, and more will be closing soon. The work is all going to China."

"But why?"

"People can work for less over there, a lot less. Don't ask me how."

Back in the city center, and all out of hope, I went into the church next to the soup kitchen. I took off my hat as I entered. Off to the side, I found the shrine of the Virgin, with many candles burning. I dropped a ten-centavo coin into the metal box and lit a candle of my own. I thought of my family and fought to stay in control of myself. I looked into the face of Our Lady of Guadalupe. As always, she was looking to the side. She's looking at my mother, I thought. I comforted myself with the story of the miracle. It was an

Indian the Lady had appeared to on several occasions. It was on the robe of the poorest of the poor that she left her famous image.

I said a prayer and left the church with hope burning once again in my heart, at least a flicker. I sat on the broad steps outside and watched the people on the street below. Most of them weren't really from here, I knew. Like me, they had been stranded in the whirlpool that was Nogales, going round and round while the river of humanity passed us by, streaming north.

Many were in a lot worse shape than me, especially the old people. Here came a man who wasn't old but had a bad limp. He was leaning on a walking stick. Tall, skinny, and shaggy-haired, he walked stooped over, eyes on the cobbles. His backpack, stuffed full, made me wonder if he was a mojado. One look at his face, and I had to look away. He had been given a terrible beating, and not very long ago. When I looked again, I noticed that one of his eyelids was frozen in place, half open and half closed.

I remembered the sleepy eyelid of the man on the bus, my lone wolf. I took a better look and I couldn't believe it. Same backpack, same black baseball cap, even the same snap-button shirt, only now it had bloodstains on it. Same man! What in the world?

I followed him down the street. Miguel, I remembered, that was his name. Some cholos here in Nogales must have beaten him up. Whatever had happened, his fully loaded pack meant that he was about to cross the border.

This might be the Virgin's answer to my prayer, I told myself. Here was someone I knew, sort of. I had no choice but to follow, and see what this would come to.

Sleepy Eye's path led to the busy bus terminal. He bought a ticket—I didn't know where to. I had no money to buy a ticket.

Miguel limped outside and waited on the platform. I was careful not to let him catch me watching. He boarded a second-class bus marked for Agua Prieta. Where that was, I had no idea. I stood there wondering if this was the end. The bus driver was planted on the curb right by the door, taking the tickets. How could I get past him?

From the cover of a column, I waited for my chance. I thought of Julio, who always believed that a chance would arrive. I just had to be ready.

All the passengers seemed to be aboard. I was sure that the driver was about to follow, take his seat, and shut the door. Instead he looked at his watch and stepped aside. He lit a cigarette and chatted with another driver on the platform.

His back wasn't turned long, just long enough for me to glide aboard.

12

Miguel

MIGUEL DIDN'T NOTICE ME coming down the aisle. I took a seat in the next-to-last row. The driver climbed aboard and gave a quick look toward the back of the crowded bus. He didn't notice me either. I was soon rolling up and over the hills, out of Nogales.

The bus went flying south like a bullet—wrong direction. I was afraid that my lone wolf had given up after all, and was heading home. Where would that leave me? Finally the driver turned sharply left. I asked the woman at my elbow if she lived in Agua Prieta, where this bus was going. She said she did. I asked if it was anywhere near the border. She said it was right on the border, across from Douglas, Arizona.

Late afternoon, we arrived in Agua Prieta. I kept a close eye on Miguel. Most people were getting off, and I was sure he would, too, but he stayed put. So did I, slouching in the back and hoping

I wouldn't attract any attention. The bus filled with new people, and minutes later was flying along the border to the east.

No metal wall separated the countries here, only the barbed wire fence my father had once described, a simple cattle fence. A green-and-white Migra truck was raising dust on a dirt road hugging the other side. In the next minute I saw a second truck, then a third one. They were everywhere. The Border Patrol, not the fence, was going to be the problem.

At his own window, Miguel was also paying close attention. With the sun setting behind us, the bus left the desert plain and began to climb the foothills of a mountain range. My lobo was studying the mountainsides, like he'd seen them before and was looking for something in particular. Suddenly, he stood and started up the aisle. I would have followed if he hadn't left his pack and walking stick behind.

The foothills were full of sharp curves. As Miguel approached the driver, he had to brace to keep his feet. A bit of green showed from his fist. I didn't see the money pass hands, but I could tell he was paying the driver for an unscheduled stop. My throat, suddenly, was dry as rawhide.

Miguel returned down the aisle. A minute later, we were slowing down. Drowsy passengers opened their eyes. Miguel had his pack and walking stick, and was bracing his way forward. I grabbed my own pack and did the same. With a hiss, the bus came to a complete stop. "Go with God," someone called from behind. Miguel stepped down to the shoulder of the pavement. The bus was pulling out before he realized that someone else had gotten off. He was caught by surprise, and unhappy, but he didn't even take a good look at me. Fast as he could, he started down a steep embankment, then up a dry wash.

The wash was a fan of sand and gravel at the mouth of a narrow canyon. As soon as Miguel reached the canyon, with the highway out of sight, he stopped to lean on his stick and scowl in my direction. I stayed well behind. Twice more, he turned and scowled. What did I care? I wasn't asking him to be my friend.

It got dark fast. The stars came out, but the moonlight was blocked by the canyon walls. There was barely enough light to avoid the rocks and cactus. Before long Miguel came to a dry waterfall. He climbed around it. At a fork in the canyon, he veered left. It was easier to see now with the steep, lower reaches of the canyon behind us. The moon was unblocked and half full. It had been growing. Two weeks had gone by since I left home, but it felt like a whole lot longer.

I followed Miguel up a shallow wash. It led to a fence with seven strands of barbed wire. I waited for him to climb over it, but he just stood there. Resting, I thought, but then he waved me toward him. I stayed where I was. He waved me forward again. This time I went.

In the moonlight, his swollen face was a terrible thing to see — broken nose, jaw askew, stitches above his right eye. He didn't say a thing, just glared at me.

I pointed to the barbed wire fence. "Is that the border?"

"It is," he said with disdain.

"So, that's the States on the other side."

"Isn't that what I just said? Go ahead, cross the wire. What are you waiting for?"

For the first time I noticed his front teeth. The bottom ones were freshly missing. His wounds and his pain and his sleepy eye unnerved me. He was truly terrifying to look at. "You're the kid from the bus," he said. "The bus from Silao, then the one from Guadalajara. You sat next to me. Started talking about green cards."

"And got thrown off."

"Don't tell me your troubles. I got my own."

"It looks like we both had a rough time in Nogales."

He didn't seem to have heard me. He cocked his head to one side and told me to say it again, which I did.

He motioned toward his face. "You talking about this? This didn't happen in Nogales. It happened on the other side."

"Oh," I said. "You've already been across? This is your second try?"

"I don't have time for this conversation," he growled. "Go ahead, pass me. Can't you see I'm moving slow?"

"I don't know the way."

"Go north, good luck."

"I have a feeling it's not that easy."

"Whatever you say. Just quit following me like a dog. It's getting on my nerves."

"I'll follow farther back, where you won't see me."

He raised the stick and shook it. "Do I need to beat you like a dog?"

"If you do, I'll still follow. You know where you're going and I don't. I might be able to help you, Miguel."

"How in the devil do you know my name?"

"From the bus, as you were showing your identification to the police. What if I carry the heavy things from your pack? You could get some of the weight off your legs. Don't worry about me running off with your food. I have my own, and a jug of water."

"Listen, kid, I can't afford to make any more mistakes. I have a wife and four small children back home. Walk your own road and bear your own load—that's my motto. Any little mistake of yours would give me away."

"Then keep me close, where you can make sure I won't make any."

"You are a persistent one, aren't you?"

"Persistence is one thing I have a lot of."

"You're like a fly in my face, and just as annoying."

With that, the man slipped the pack off his back. It took me a second to realize he had given in. He pulled all the food out of his pack, quite a variety. All I had left in my own was two tins. I showed Miguel my can of pork so it wouldn't get confused with one of his.

"That's all you've got?" he barked.

"And a can of peppers—I don't eat much. By the way, my name is Victor Flores."

"Born in Chiapas, as you told the police. Raised in Guanajuato."

"You believed me?"

"Of course. When 'Camino de Guanajuato' was playing on the first bus, you cried a large puddle."

"That much?"

"Nearly. Throw out that flashlight. It will give us away."

"It's gone. There, all packed. Can I help you over the fence?"

"Why, when it's been knocked down right over there?"

"Oh," I said, "I didn't see."

"Open your eyes wide, Victor Flores. I do a lot of walking in the dark. And don't speak unless you are spoken to. I can't afford to have you give me away."

"You can count on me, Miguel."

"I'm not going to get caught again. We're going high, where the bighorn sheep go."

I fell in behind and started walking. Three times that night, from high above, we watched mojados winding their way single-file up the canyon bottoms behind their coyotes. From a distance, they looked like centipedes, which is what Miguel called them. "Cut off the head," he said, "and the body will die."

The fourth time, there was something different about the centipede. Miguel brought out a pair of binoculars. He took a long look. "Their backpacks are huge and all the same," he reported. "Those are mules. Drug runners."

Once the moon set, it got so dark I couldn't see my feet. I fell several times, filling my hands with tiny cactus needles. I didn't cry out.

Dawn came, and we took off our packs. "Sit on my right side," Miguel directed. "Always on my right side."

"Why is that?"

"Because I can't hear out of my left ear. Haven't you noticed?"

"Sort of."

"As the Americans would say, you're not the sharpest knife in the drawer."

"I do my best."

He threw me a needle-nose pliers. I caught them, looking confused. "For those cactus needles," he explained. "But first, find some tortillas and cheese, and grab your can of chilies. Here's a can opener."

I drained the water off the chili peppers and spread the food on a rock. My hunger was painful. Trying not to look at his food — once was enough for him to describe me as a dog — I reached for one of my peppers.

"Going north to join your father?" my guide said gruffly, as he reached for a tortilla and broke off some cheese, then grabbed a pepper.

"I'm on my own."

"Looking for excitement, is that it?"

"Looking to support my mother, my sisters, and my little brother."

"Eat!" he ordered approvingly.

I nodded and helped myself, but I didn't say thanks. This man would hate it if I groveled.

I thought he would press me about my father. He didn't. "How's your family been getting by up till now?" he asked instead.

"I've been farming—raising corn."

"I used to raise corn myself. That's no way to make a living."

"How long have you been working in El Norte?"

"Since I was nineteen. Eight years."

"Always crossing alone?"

"This is my third time alone. Like everyone else, I used to pay the coyotes. Until I was in a group they abandoned. It was in May—hot as a blacksmith's fire. Half of us died. Never again will I pay them a thing. You know what the coyotes call their customers these days?"

"Pollos, I have heard." I was thinking of Rico, the others from the village, and all the men who came before, like our fathers.

"Chickens, that's right. Cooked chickens, no less. And the coyotes have another cute name for their underlings who actually guide people across the desert—polleros."

"Chicken wranglers?"

"They think that's funny. Meanwhile, we are supposed to regard them as heroes. They are scum, my friend. I would rather die than pay them a fortune, only to have them betray me at the drop of a hat."

"When you were deported a few days ago . . . had the Migra kept you in jail?"

"Soon as I got sewed up, they deported me. The jails were too crowded."

"I've heard that the American jails are really bad."

"Are you kidding? Three meals a day, and lie around and watch TV? You must be thinking of our Mexican jails. I've been in American jail—twice."

I hesitated. "Did the Border Patrol do that to you, then, before they let you go?"

"This? My head, my ribs, my knee? People talk about the Border Patrol doing such things, but I've never seen it. They catch you, they hand you a bottle of clean drinking water and they put you in their air-conditioned perrera."

"Perrera—what is that?" I was done eating, and was pulling cactus needles with the pliers.

"Dog wagon—truck with a holding cell in the back. It's what we mojados call them, because the Border Patrol are like dog-catchers."

"If it wasn't the Border Patrol, who beat you up so bad?"

"Vigilantes. I had always heard about mojados crossing east of Agua Prieta, on the flats. You saw that stretch from the bus. It looks easy. Hundreds do it every night. I got past the strip of government land, where the Border Patrol are so thick, but then I got caught crossing the private ranches. Lots of coyotes lead their mojados through there. Some groups get caught, some don't."

"By vigilantes?"

"Yes—the private militias, who are angry with their government for not stopping the flood. It didn't use to be like this. The ranchers used to put out water for people, before there were so many of us, before the coyotes started smashing down their fences, breaking into their houses, stealing their vehicles . . . times have changed."

"These vigilantes, what do they do?"

"Catch people and turn them over to the Border Patrol. But some of them, as I found out, have sick minds. They come from far off to dress up like soldiers, carry guns like soldiers, and commit crimes for which they will never be punished."

I cringed, imagining what must have happened to Miguel. "They beat you up, and then they turned you over?"

"They would have been arrested for what they did to me. They just dumped me in the road like a piece of meat."

"I'm sorry, Miguel."

"Don't be sorry for me, or for yourself, either, when the bad things happen. You have to stay strong for your family. You have to be a man."

13

Land of Opportunity

I THOUGHT WE WOULD hole up when daylight came, but I was wrong. We walked on and on. As long as we kept to the highest and most rugged places, Miguel thought we wouldn't be seen. The day warmed and stayed comfortable. At a trickling spring, we found water.

The second night got so cold, only the work of the hiking kept us from freezing. The moon was throwing plenty of light. We had left the scaly Guadalupe Mountains behind and were into the Peloncillos, strewn with giant boulders.

Miguel would often pull out his map and show me where we were. "Look how far we've come," he said in the middle of the night. "We've crossed from New Mexico to Arizona and back into New Mexico."

My answer was a yawn. I was asleep on my feet.

Ten minutes later, I fell into a clump of cactus and started some rocks rolling. A herd of animals we didn't even know were there went bounding away in the moonlight. Bighorn sheep, Miguel said they were. The night grew quiet again, but the desert mountains were far from empty. It was never long before something made the hair stand up on the back of my neck—coyotes, owls, who-knows-what.

Daylight brought the honking of thousands of northbound geese, who made it look like we were moving at the speed of ants. Miguel had his map out and was looking for a way down to the narrow San Bernardino Valley, in sight to the west but not yet in reach. We would have to cross that valley before we could climb into the high Chiricahua Mountains on the other side.

"What about this deep canyon right below us?" I asked. "Bet we could find a way to drop into it, and it leads to the valley."

"Skeleton Canyon, it's called. Look here, it has a road up it. We might run into Border Patrol. Let's keep looking. How did you hurt your head, anyway?"

"Train," I said. "The doctor said that the stitches will fall out when they're ready."

"Stay away from trains," Miguel grunted.

We kept going north. Above Skull Canyon, Miguel spread out the map on a slab of granite. It was broad daylight, but Miguel was pretty sure we were out of the reach of the Border Patrol. My guide showed me how to get a rough idea of north by the position of the sun and the time of day. I already knew, but I didn't tell him so. Always lay the map out, he said, so it's pointing north. He started talking about the patches of color on the map, the different ownership of land the colors stood for. My eyes drifted to a nearby rock where a spiny lizard with bright orange markings was doing push-ups. Somehow its attitude reminded me of Rico. I had to smile.

"Well?" said Miguel irritably.

"I was just wondering why they do that."

"To attract the girls, of course. I used to do it when I was your age."

My laugh was cut short as Miguel slapped the map with the side of his hand. "Why do you think I am showing you all this?"

I was taken aback. "It's a good thing to know, I guess."

"What is your plan? Let someone else lead the way and hope for the best? Well, the best seldom happens. Everything I tell you is in case we get separated!"

"That's not going to happen, Miguel."

"What do you know! It could happen in a hundred ways. Then where would you be?"

As we came down the slopes of the Peloncillos, we found warmer temperatures and springtime. The hillsides were washed blue and red with wildflowers. The rocks were sprinkled with golden poppies. Hummingbirds shot back and forth like arrows.

Miguel was warmer too, more cheerful. He seemed to actually be enjoying my company. We laughed at the clumsy bees smacking into our hats. In Skull Canyon, we drank from the creek like camels, filled our water jugs, and bathed. My bandage fell off. I washed my hair with a bar of soap and also washed some underwear.

Miguel took a switchblade out of his pack, opened it, folded it shut, opened it, folded it shut.

"Have you ever had to use it?" I asked.

"Many times," he replied. Miguel opened the knife once more. With a laugh, he began to trim his fingernails.

"I didn't know my guide had a sense of humor," I said.

"Life has many surprises, my friend."

It was enjoyable to rest and to eat under a tall cottonwood, newly leafed out and spring green. We were going to wait for the sun to dry our laundry spread out on the rocks. Miguel was feeling so good, he sang a ballad about a gunfighter who raided across the border with Pancho Villa.

"Your father," Miguel said after the song. "I have the feeling he is dead."

I gave a painful nod.

"Crossing the desert? At work in El Norte?"

"At work. In South Carolina."

"Doing something dangerous, I suppose. We never refuse. How long ago?"

"Four years."

"Before the famous September 11, then. Before the Americans got so afraid of terrorists, and hired so many more Border Patrol. Probably your father was able to come home every year for the holidays."

"From Christmas until the middle of March."

"A couple months a year was all you had of him. Same for my

kids. I have two girls and two boys."

"You're brave to come home."

"No, just stupid. Hardly anybody from my village risks it anymore. I would do anything to bring my wife and my little ones across, if only I could. How I would love for my kids to have the advantages of the States. Kids can even go to school without having to prove they are legal. The Americans are generous that way."

"My friend who left before me calls El Norte the land of opportunity."

"It is, if you're willing to work hard. In the States, it's possible to start from the ground and reach the top of the tree. In Mexico, if you are born poor, there are no branches within reach, and the trunk is coated with lard."

"My friend—his name is Rico—was born poor, yet his father built him a ladder. Until a couple of weeks ago, he was in school in Silao. He could have learned a trade and got a good job, yet he ran away to the States."

"Who's to blame him? In El Norte, there's a lot more fruit on the tree, which reminds me of something I should warn you about. When you make money up there, it's very easy to spend it. To waste it on things that are senseless."

"I'll send it home, all that I can."

"Good."

To my surprise, Miguel said we were in no hurry to move on. After all the hard walking, we finally got some sleep.

Miguel nudged me awake in the middle of the afternoon, and we climbed to a lookout. The San Bernardino Valley lay below, nearly in our laps. Across the valley, the towering Chiricahua Mountains looked close enough to touch. I could even see the shapes of the tall trees blanketing their upper slopes.

Miguel spread out the map. We were back in Arizona, this time to stay. For the first time, he told me where we were going, and how we were going to get there. His route ran the length of the Chiricahua Mountains and then the Dos Cabezas. Only when we were within a mile of what he called the interstate highway, at a town called Willcox, were we going to come down out of the mountains.

It was unbelievable, what Miguel had in mind. By the time we got there we would have walked all the way from Mexico to the big highway running across southern Arizona. "How many miles?" I asked.

"Don't even think about the distance. It can be done, that's all that counts."

Our destination was a blank spot on the map along a gravel road north of Willcox. The illegals called it The Skinny Dog. La Perra Flaca was a place where mojados lived ten or fifteen to a trailer and were met every morning by labor contractors who took them to work in the onions and the chilies.

"Once you get north of the interstate," Miguel explained, "the Border Patrol doesn't bother you anymore unless you get into trouble or an accident."

"I can work there too—with you?"

"Why do you think I'm telling you all this?"

"I can't tell you how happy this makes me feel."

"Well, you never know how long the work will last. We'll work there until you can send a money order home. Then we'll move on to other states."

"Why not stay there?"

"The work dries up. Anyway, we can do better. In case we get separated, I'll look for you at La Perra Flaca. Your nose will tell you when you're getting close. The sewage overflows."

Miguel passed the binoculars and had me scan the paved road that ran the length of the San Bernardino Valley. We were going to cross it a mile north of Apache, where the valley narrowed to eight miles. We had to cross the flats before we could find cover in the Chiricahua Mountains.

"I can see a gas station," I said. "And a few trailers. Where's Apache?"

"That's it."

"I see two perreras."

"The dogcatchers flock to those convenience stores for the coffee that is like battery acid."

"A white jeep with green markings is driving in."

"More Border Patrol."

"Maybe all the patrolmen will be there tonight."

"Somehow I doubt that."

"Look, it's starting to get cloudy. The moon won't give us away."

"They have night-vision goggles."

"I see three more perreras—two on the side of the highway and one on a dirt road dragging something behind."

"Tires hooked together. Every day, they erase the old footprints so they can see the new ones."

Miguel took the binoculars back and looked some more. He said that the desert was rigged with motion sensors and hidden cameras—ordinary cameras for the daytime, heat cameras for the night. Even in pitch dark the Border Patrol could see you moving through the desert by the heat of your body. In Apache or nearby, a man was watching dozens of TV screens. Higher overhead than we could see, an airplane that could fly without a pilot might be watching us right now.

"They sure go to a lot of trouble," I said. "It's a crazy world, no?"

"You got that right. They say that one out of every ten citizens of Mexico is living in the States. Think if they ever rounded us all up. Who would do all the work? Are they willing to pick the fruits and the vegetables to fill their grocery stores? How much would their food cost without us to harvest it? I tell you, they would miss us badly. As for our own country, think if we weren't able send all this money back to our families."

"It's my family's only chance."

"Listen carefully now . . . when we cross to the Chiricahuas tonight, we have to be very alert. If we're unlucky, we'll have to run fast as antelopes."

"But you can't do that."

"In my case it was just an expression."

"I wish there weren't so many Border Patrol."

"I didn't expect this many this far north. It's a sign that wets are hiking greater distances than ever. It means we'll have to go higher in the mountains than I was thinking. Up into the tall trees. It'll be cold up there."

"Better cold than hot, no? You know what, I predict we won't have trouble with the Border Patrol tonight."

"I'm happy to hear you say that, but talking about bulls is not the same as facing them in the ring."

"That was one of my father's sayings!"

"Your father was a wise man."

For comfort, I turned my face to the late sun. High above, the vultures were wheeling in circles.

"Those vultures are Mexicans," Miguel said. "Migratory workers, indocumentados. Yet no one throws them in the zoo for lack of documents. Well, I'm afraid it's time for us to get going. Even the best horse needs to be spurred. Did your father used to say that one?"

"No, but how about this: 'Once mounted on a horse, one must hang on when he bucks.'"

"Good advice. Keep it in mind, Victor."

14

You'll Need These

A T DUSK WE BEGAN the crossing of the valley. Keeping low as quail, we threaded our way through prickly pear and yuccas. Miguel began to limp faster on his bad knee, keeping the lights of Apache on his left. Close on his heels, I picked up a shoeful of cactus needles but didn't say anything.

Up ahead, there were cars on the highway, not many, but sometimes they came in bunches. When we got close, Miguel hid me in the brush, then bellied up to the shoulder of the road. He crossed first while I waited. When Miguel's whistle finally came, I scrambled up the shoulder and darted across. After days on dirt, rock, and sand, the pavement under my feet felt strange.

I ran into the cover of the scrub on the far side of the highway. "Stay down," I heard Miguel call. Cars were coming from both directions. At last there was nothing but quiet, and Miguel whistled again. I found him and we crouched together in the brush.

"It's really dark," I said. I was shivering, and not just from the cold. "Not much moonlight is getting through those clouds."

"The clouds are thin," he scoffed. "Plenty of light."

"It seems farther to the mountains than it did before," I said. I couldn't help it, I was trembling. "Are you sure there isn't another way?"

"There are hundreds. You could cross at Naco, and try to find the Americans in Bisbee who hide people in their homes and sometimes even drive them to Tucson or Phoenix. You could cross into the Huachuca Mountains, the Patagonias, or the Pajaritos. You could try Santa Cruz Valley, the Altar Valley, the Indian reservation, the Organ Pipe cactus park, the Cabeza Prieta—"

"Enough," I said. "I'm sorry I questioned you. We wouldn't be here if you didn't think this was best."

"Only four more miles and we'll be in those mountains, compadre."

"I just wish it wasn't so dark."

Seconds later, we came to a dirt road parallel to the highway. Miguel whispered instructions in my ear. I crossed first. Miguel, walking backward, erased our tracks with a small piece of brush.

With that we headed into the open, the Chiricahua Mountains four miles away. The valley floor was mostly grasses sprinkled with bushes and ocotillo—no places to hide as far as I could see. I felt safe as a caterpillar crawling through a yard full of chickens. What about the heat cameras and all the other Migra tricks? Miguel went as fast as he could on his stick, wincing with the pain but

103

showing none of the fear I still couldn't shake.

Beyond the clouds, there were stars, like candles burning. The idea of the candles helped. I could see my mother in the village church, lighting a candle for me in front of the Lady. I saw my family sitting around the table, Chuy making one of his chango faces. He really did look like a little monkey.

The land began to rise as we started up a plain of gravel. The bushes were knee-high—still no cover. As I soon discovered, Miguel had a plan all along. He'd been marching toward a snaking line of mesquite bushes that turned out to mark the bank of a dry streambed cutting through the valley from the mountains. When we dropped ten or more feet to the bottom of the arroyo, I felt a lot safer.

We followed the twists and turns of the wash until we came to a sharp corner dammed by logs and rocks. We had no choice but to climb out. Miguel led the way up. He crawled out on his knees so as not to attract attention, and I did the same.

The clouds had parted in front of the moon. It was more than half full, and shining much too bright. "We'll drop back in soon as we can," Miguel whispered. He pointed to the sprinklings of oak and juniper trees on higher ground, on the lap of the mountains. "Once we get inside those, we're invisible."

His words were still hanging in the air. I happened to be looking back toward the highway when the headlights of a vehicle suddenly came on between the highway and us. They were pointed in our direction. "Miguel," I yelped.

"Don't like the looks of that," Miguel muttered. "Their instruments might be onto us. Keep low."

"We've been so careful. It must be someone else they're after."

The headlights began to move. I could see the shape of the vehicle. "Perrera," I said, as it gained more and more speed, heading our way.

"Bad luck," Miguel grunted, and took off hobbling on his stick. Half a minute later, he found a way back down into the dry creekbed. On my way over the steep embankment, I slipped and banged my arm. No matter. I caught up with him, and that was all that counted.

It was slow going in the wash, but we would be spotted if we climbed out. We made some progress, but then I thought I heard the perrera. We stopped and listened. "Holy mother of God!" I said. The dog wagon was over our left shoulders and not very far behind.

Miguel clapped me on the shoulder. "You have the advantage, Victor. They're wearing heavy body armor. You can run faster than they can."

We heard their truck stopping, then the sound of a slamming door. We looked back and saw a patrolman at the top of the bank, about a hundred yards behind us. The Migra had his gun drawn, and was on his way down to the bottom of the arroyo. Where were the clouds when we needed them?

"He'll find our footprints," I whispered.

"Follow quietly," Miguel whispered back.

We'd barely gotten started when a second patrolman appeared at the top of the bank, much closer. No question he had seen us. Miguel tried to run on the walking stick. The patrolman yelled for us to stop and give ourselves up.

Miguel took off, desperately fast. All I knew was, this couldn't be the end. I picked my way through the rubble along the rocky floor of the wash. I caught up as Miguel was climbing out on the bank opposite the two Border Patrol.

We lost track of them, but they hadn't lost track of us. Just when I thought they had decided to let us go, their vehicle fired up and started following along the other side of the arroyo. As long as there was no way for them to cross, we were going to be okay. Ahead, the oaks and junipers grew thicker, taller. Just beyond them, the steep, brushy slopes offered good cover. Hope began to run strong. The mountains were close, so close. Suddenly mindless of Miguel, I sprinted ahead.

A sharp cry came from behind. Miguel was down.

I ran back to him. "I'll be okay in a minute," he said. "Lie flat next to me in these rocks. Let's hope they can't get across."

"Look, thick clouds covering the moon!"

Suddenly it was a whole lot darker, and we had hope again.

I waited on my belly. The engine sounded different, muffled. "They're in the bottom of the wash," Miguel said. "They found a place to get across."

The Border Patrol truck climbed out of the arroyo, not a hundred yards behind us. The patrolmen got out, looking all around.

Neither of us moved a muscle. From that distance, in the dark, we were just two more rocks, or so we were hoping. Fortunately their headlights weren't on us.

Then something weird—two pairs of circular eyes glowing green in the dark. "Night-vision goggles," Miguel whispered. "Help me up, quick!"

I did, but he was shaky on his feet and needed steadying. We looked over our shoulders into the blinding headlights of the Border Patrol. "Hurry," Miguel told himself as he took off, but he had hurt himself and couldn't go any faster.

The ground was strewn with rocks, which promised to be our salvation. The Border Patrol couldn't drive any faster than Miguel could hobble. We managed to close the distance to the trees by half, and were entering a boulder field.

Finally the perrera ground to a halt, its headlights frozen in place. "It's too rough for them to keep going," I said. "They're going to let us go."

"I'll believe that when I see it." Miguel rested on my shoulder as we waited to see if they were going to chase us on foot.

"Please," Miguel murmured. "Show us mercy."

It wasn't to be. The patrolmen were coming on. One of them had a rifle, or maybe it was a shotgun.

Fast as he could, Miguel hobbled on. The oaks and the junipers were no more than three hundred yards away. Miguel looked back toward the patrolmen. Suddenly he dropped his pack to the ground and tore it open. I had no idea what he was doing. Miguel pulled out his map, grabbed the can opener, shoved them at me. "You'll need these lighters to start fires," he said. "Here, take this roll of parachute cord. Go high."

"Miguel . . ."

He slapped his switchblade into my hand. "You'll need this too, to make kindling. Let's go, let's go!"

Fast as I could, I stowed these things, and we took off again, Miguel trying to run. After a fashion, like a crippled dog, he was able to. A glance over my shoulder, and I could see that the patrolmen were running too, and they were closing in. Miguel stumbled and almost went down.

"Grab hold of my shoulder!" I cried.

"They'll catch both of us!"

Miguel held back, and then he stopped in his tracks. "Now is the time," Miguel said. "Run as fast as you can."

"Not without you! Let them deport us. We'll start over."

"They'll split us up. Listen, Victor, you can make it to La Perra Flaca."

"Without you?"

"If you find work, wait for me there. I'll be along."

I froze.

"Go, go!" Miguel screamed.

I took off running. A glance over my shoulder, and I saw Miguel following as best as he could. The patrolmen were practically on him when Miguel tripped and went down.

I halted in my tracks. They were handcuffing Miguel. "Stop!"

one of them called after me. "Stop, please. Sit down right where you are!"

I ran. A look back and I could see that the more slender of the two was chasing me.

The patrolman was fast, very fast, even with his body armor, and he was gaining ground. But I had more reason to run than he ever would. I ran toward the trees with everything I had. My lungs opened up and my eyes widened to see like an owl. I put my fear aside and ran, ran for my family.

I didn't look back again. I ran into a thicket of catclaw mesquite. The catclaw tore my cheeks and my hands, but it didn't stop me. I could hear the patrolman panting to keep up. I led him deeper into the thorny scrub, where he might not put up with the punishment.

At last I was out of the thorns and under the dense and friendly cover of oak and juniper. I was pretty sure I'd lost the Migra.

Finally, I stopped. I threw myself on the ground. I waited, listening for the slightest sound. For a long time there was nothing but the night insects and the hooting of an owl. I was alone.

15

Too High Up

T HE NIGHT WAS COLD. I passed the dark hours burrowed in the oak brush and shivering in my blanket. My mind kept going over everything that had happened, especially Miguel giving me even more from his pack to go along with his food. Did he really believe I could make it on my own?

Dawn on the high Chiricahuas made them look like a fortress of cliffs and pinnacles. How was I supposed to reach those tall pines up around the peaks? "Go high," Miguel had commanded at the last.

Up and moving, I was funneled into a deep canyon with a live stream. Following the stream up to where it started seemed like the only way I could reach the big trees, where there would be open ground and easier walking. Twice I left the water to climb and see if the Border Patrol was after me. No sign of them. Too much trouble to catch one person?

Late morning I stopped by a clear pool under cottonwoods that were only beginning to bud. I drank from the pool and ate two sticks of jerky. I was thinking about bathing in the pool but the day was cloudy and cold, nothing like the day before.

I got out Miguel's map. I found the Chiricahua Mountains and the Dos Cabezas, the freeway, and Willcox, Arizona. I found the blank spot where La Perra Flaca was supposed to be. On a slab of granite, I took stock of everything I had: blanket, water jug, a roll of toilet paper, a change of clothes, Miguel's parachute cord, his knife and lighters, two boxes of cookies, three packs of jerky, four tins of tuna fish, and a box of hard, thick crackers.

I repacked, then studied the map some more. A dirt road ran east and west through the middle of the Chiricahuas. Until I crossed it I wouldn't really know where I was. If I climbed high, then kept heading north, I would cross that road. How I missed Miguel. "You have to be a man," I kept hearing him say. "You have to be a man."

Staring at that road on the map wasn't going to bring it any closer. It was time to start climbing again.

The cottonwoods along the stream gave way to trees I'd never seen before. By early afternoon, after scrambling around three waterfalls, I had reached the level of the cliffs and the pinnacles.

One more push, and I climbed into the tall pines. The walking came easier. I tracked the stream to its beginnings, a mere trickle. I drank and filled my jug. The wind was out of the west, the tree limbs beginning to sway. The clouds were thickening. Dirty snowbanks here and there gave me something new to worry about. Could it snow again? March was almost over, but what if winter wasn't?

Fast as I could, I pushed on. I steered toward a mountain to the northwest, the highest in the range. The map called it Chiricahua

Peak, almost ten thousand feet high. By late afternoon the giant pines were creaking and groaning in the wind. My jacket never felt so thin. A dark cloudbank was racing in from the west, and I could feel the moisture coming. I knew I better get down some, and not on the windy side of the mountains.

I found a place on the protected side and spent the rest of the daylight gathering firewood and making a shelter with the knife and the parachute cord. I made my lean-to large, big enough to keep myself and the wood dry. I covered the firewood with a thick layer of branches. By the time I was done, the wind was shrieking through the snags and the crags, and the temperature was dropping fast. I was wearing everything I had, and still I was cold.

Miguel would have been proud of this camp, I thought, and of this shelter, built on a well-drained spot under the trees and close to a small creek. At dusk I made a ring of stones under the high side of the shelter and got a fire going. For now there was nothing to do but wait and see what the weather would do.

I wasn't long finding out. Soon after dark, it started snowing hard, the flakes large as peso coins. It snowed all night as I stoked the fire to keep from freezing. I thought about the earth warming back home, the seeds sprouting in my mother's vegetable garden. I was glad they couldn't picture me like this.

By dawn, a foot of snow covered the ground—a beautiful sight, but strange and scary. The morning brought patches of blue sky, but they didn't last. It started to snow hard again—would it ever quit? All the while, I had to keep ranging farther to find dead branches for the fire. My sneakers were hopelessly soaked, my feet freezing whenever they were away from the fire. By the time the storm ended, the snow was up to my knees. I wondered if Miguel knew it could get this bad up here. What would he do?

Miguel would wait. The snow will melt soon, I kept telling myself. Hiking through this much of it was impossible. I passed the time going over and over the exact address of the Western Union in Silao where I would wire the money home. I had to believe I could still make that happen.

The next day brought blue skies but no melting. The day after that, finally, warmer air arrived. The snow slumped. It took another day for enough to melt to set me free. I got going, but without much hope. My food was nearly gone.

It was hard walking in the slush, and my feet were numb. I'd never known how much cold feet could hurt. I began to have the strangest feeling—that I was being followed. I would stop every so often to look back and see if anyone was there, but no one was. I felt as alone as a man walking on the moon, small as an ant, utterly helpless.

I kept walking, yet couldn't shake the feeling. The hackles went up on the back of my neck. I turned around fast—nothing, nothing there. I told myself to pretend I was walking at my father's side. In a way it was true. He would always be with me. "Everyone is master of their own fear," I heard him saying, and that helped.

Farther on, I got even more suspicious. I might have heard something. I whipped around quickly, and there it was, no more than twenty feet away—a huge tawny cat. The puma snarled to find itself discovered, and went into a crouch. Long as my arm, its tail was waving slowly back and forth.

There were pumas back home, but people rarely laid eyes on one. They preyed on deer and stray goats, and had a reputation for following people at a distance. This one had come close, much too close. Carmita, the old woman who rang the village bells, liked to tell the story of one carrying off a child when she was young, in some other village. I hadn't really believed her. I believed her now. Without a doubt, this animal had been stalking me.

The puma coiled, tail going faster and faster. It was about to spring, and I was wishing I was a whole lot bigger.

I didn't really think about what to do. I only knew I couldn't turn and run. My hand went to my pocket for the switchblade. "I am the jaguar!" I screamed. "The mighty tigre! You are nothing but a mountain lion! Get out of here, or I'll rip you limb from limb. I'll cut you inside out!"

The puma wasn't so sure it wanted a piece of me after all. I reached for a big stick, a piece of a shattered tree limb that the wind had brought down, and started waving it around and around like a crazy man.

The lion turned around, and with a last look over its shoulder, vanished into the forest. I went to look at its tracks. They were bigger than my fist. I found a different stick—a perfect club—and kept going. It took long time before I wasn't looking as much behind as ahead, and just as long for my heart to quit racing.

By the middle of the afternoon I was on a high ridge with few trees. Chiricahua Peak was straight ahead. I was thinking that less snow would remain on its west side on account of the wind and the sun. I had just made up my mind to head that way when I heard the chop of a helicopter. It was so loud it had to be close. Where, exactly, I couldn't tell.

Here it came, rushing up from below. It was right there, hovering just off the ridge, with me caught out in the open.

No doubt about it, I'd been seen.

I ran downhill, toward the beginning of a canyon and the nearest trees. The helicopter followed. It was white with green markings, and it was making a terrible wind and noise.

It was a hard run but I reached trees too thick for the helicopter to land. They could still see me, though. The Border Patrol hovered above as I bent over double, gasping for breath. I wondered what would come next. Were they going to find a landing place and send men after me?

Instead, they dropped something, a plastic jar.

It could be food, I thought. It could be anything. Cautiously, I unscrewed the lid. Inside was a message weighted with sand. In hastily scribbled Spanish it read, STAY WHERE YOU ARE. WE ARE HERE TO HELP YOU.

They wanted to help, but there was no promise here that they wouldn't deport me.

What would Miguel do?

The answer came easy. He wouldn't give up. I looked up at the man with the helmet who was leaning out of the helicopter. He was holding a white metal box with a red cross on it. I shook my head, then ran down into the canyon where the slopes were steep and covered with trees thick as dog hair.

16

What Might Have Been

IN THE MORNING I ATE the last of the jerky. By now I should have been in the Dos Cabezas Mountains. I was nearly out of food, and no more than halfway from the border to La Perra Flaca. Somehow, I had to find a shortcut. The map showed a small lake at the foot of the mountains on their western side. A road from the lake led to other roads and eventually the town of Willcox. Maybe I would get lucky and catch a ride.

A few miles down the canyon I came across footprints in the mud—lots of them, and they were fresh. The hikers seemed to be on their way out of the mountains. I guessed I was following some Americans until I found a candy wrapper with a Spanish label. It was the first in a fresh stream of trash with labels in Spanish.

Did I want to meet a group of mojados, or not?

Before long I heard voices. It was Spanish they were speaking. I edged closer, and peeked through the brush. The people were on a patch of green grass in the sunlight, some sitting and talking, others on their backs with their heads propped on their backpacks. They were muddy, ragged, and filthy—forced down from the snow like I was, and just as bad off. I counted seventeen, including six women.

The presence of the women made me hopeful. I might get some help from this group. I might get some food.

It wouldn't hurt to talk to them. Or would it?

Which was the coyote? It was impossible to tell.

I watched and I waited to see what they were going to do next. Time went by, too much time for a rest break. Were they waiting for someone?

An hour later, a bowlegged man came shuffling up the trail. He had a mustache and wore a black and red jacket—Chicago Bulls. The group stood up and gathered around to see what he would say. The way he looked at them—as if they were cattle—and the way they looked at him—with distrust—it was easy to see he was their coyote.

From a careful distance, I followed as the coyote led them down the trail. After a few miles they came to a gate in a cattle fence, and started down a rough road without tire tracks. I began to think that the mojados were about to be picked up farther down this road. I wondered if I could talk my way into joining them, wherever they were going. I would have to make some kind of deal with the coyote. Maybe he would let me pay after I found work. I was going to owe a whole lot of dollars, maybe as much as Rico's fifteen hundred.

They came to a fork in the road. Instead of leading them down-hill, on the main branch, the coyote turned uphill. I doubted this meant they were about to be picked up. Their coyote led them to a cabin on the mountainside below a boarded-up mine. I crept close to see what this was about.

The coyote was showing them that the front door was unlocked. They all started laughing. A woman pointed to a broken window. The coyote seemed to be telling them that he hadn't broken it. Again, laughter. I waited to see what they would do.

They went inside and made themselves at home. Before long, some of them came outside, eating from canned goods. I could picture them all going to jail for breaking in and stealing food. I couldn't take the chance. I had to stay on my own, like Miguel.

The road led me down to a small lake surrounded by pine trees. Guessing it was the lake on the map, I approached with the stealth of the puma. A man was fishing at the other end. A black pickup was showing between the trees.

I tried to imagine walking right up to the fisherman and asking him for a ride, to Willcox or all the way to La Perra Flaca. Whether or not I could actually speak to him—he was a gabacho—there would be no doubt in his mind that I was a wet who'd just sneaked across the border.

Why should he help me? I couldn't take the chance.

Staying hidden in the trees, I worked my way around to the parking lot. By this time the fisherman was close to where I had stood when I first spotted him. It looked like he was going to fish his way all around the lake.

The fisherman's truck was the only vehicle in the lot. I got an idea. Right behind the cab, a big toolbox spanned the bed of the truck. If the toolbox was unlocked, and had room inside. . .

Stealthily, I climbed into the back of the pickup, tried the lid of the toolbox, found it open. If I lay on my side with my knees pulled up, there would be room, just barely. I could cushion my head with my pack.

I was going to try it, but there was no reason to torture myself before it was necessary. I crept out of the pickup and climbed up the hillside. Through the trees, I kept a sharp eye on the fisherman. He started to catch fish. In the next few hours, he caught six or seven, but let them all go, which made no sense. Midafternoon, he suddenly quit, grabbed his things, and headed to his truck.

Now was the time. I hurried back to the parking lot and climbed into the back of his truck. I lifted one wing of the toolbox lid, rearranged the tools as best I could, spread my blanket across them, placed my pack for a pillow, and climbed inside. My heart was pounding like thunder.

It was an extremely tight fit. For once I was glad I was a head shorter than Rico.

I pulled down the lid until it latched. It was only then that I wondered if there was a way to open it from inside. Wildly, I began to feel around for a latch in the pitch dark. Suddenly I felt like I was buried alive. Without a doubt, this was the stupidest thing I had done in my entire life.

Calm down, I told myself, but it wasn't that easy. Here came the man's footsteps. I thought about pounding with my fists, or crying out, but I held back, almost hoping he was going to put something in the box.

I heard him open the driver door. There was a backseat in the pickup, and that's where he must have put his things. The engine fired, and he was on his way.

The gabacho drove fast on the washboard road and the pavement full of potholes that came after. I was all cramped up, and the tools under my side felt like spears. At least I had found the inside latch, put there for little children or grown fools. I only hoped that this crazy risk would pay off. The driver was probably on his way home, wherever that was. When it seemed safe, I would take a peek, then climb out and walk away. What would come after that, I had no idea.

The ride and the pain seemed to go on forever. A couple of hours, maybe, long enough to remember the Guatemalans packed into the bottom of the fruit truck, and know they had it worse. The last part was on smooth pavement. Finally, the truck stopped. I could hear the driver pumping gas and lots of traffic going by. When we started up again, there were three stops that lasted a minute or two—traffic lights? At last the driver made a sudden turn, put on the brakes, and shut the engine off. It was over. A minute or two with the opening and closing of the truck doors, and all was quiet except for cars going by every so often. It wasn't a busy street. I guessed I was in front of the driver's house. Now it was a matter of waiting, if I could stand the pain, until I felt it was safe enough to take a peek.

I never got the chance. I heard footsteps, held my breath. The bed of the truck dipped under his weight—he was climbing in. The lid of the toolbox flew open and I was looking up into the face of the gabacho. He was so surprised, the cigarette he was smoking fell from his lips.

The gabacho slammed the lid back down. "Pardon me!" I cried, but I shouldn't have expected any sympathy. I tried the latch, but by now he was sitting on the lid, and had me trapped inside. Before long he was talking to someone, someone who wasn't there. He had a cell phone, I realized. I couldn't understand a word he was saying. "Please," I kept saying. "Please let me out!"

I didn't have much longer to wait and wonder. When the lid of the toolbox opened again, it was a green uniform I was looking at. Border Patrol. I was so tied in a knot, so much in pain, the patrolman had to help me climb out of the box.

They didn't have to worry about me running down the street. I could barely stand. The Migra, whose nameplate said SANDOVAL, handed me a bottle of water. I drank it down. The gabacho fisherman said some things—he sounded very angry—as the patrolman put me in handcuffs, which meant I was going to jail. I was a prisoner, stunned and full of shame. I told the fisherman I was sorry for surprising him like that. Sandoval translated. After that the gabacho wasn't so angry anymore.

The patrolman frisked me. He reached into my pocket for the switchblade. Out with it came the plastic picture card of the Virgin. "I'll put this in your backpack," he said, almost like he was apologizing, and started to go through my things. I begged him to let me keep the map, but he said I wouldn't need it anymore.

Sandoval undid the handcuffs and locked me in the backseat of his Jeep, white with the green stripe running through the side. An iron mesh separated the backseat from the front. We drove off down the street with houses on both sides. He asked where I was from. "Guanajuato," I said. "Where is this place?"

"Willcox, Arizona."

"There is a place nearby that the mojados call La Perra Flaca?"

"Not far away."

"That's where I was trying to go. Is there any chance you would take me there?"

He didn't reply.

"Where are we going now?"

"To Tucson, to the Pima County detention center for juveniles."

"What will they do with me?"

"Hard to tell—it all depends."

"Please," I begged.

"Sorry," he said. "No more conversation."

We were soon on a highway, two lanes in each direction, then four. As we approached Tucson, the traffic was heavy. Alongside, for a minute or two, was a sleek gold car with a bunch of kids inside. The driver was a boy barely older than me. The girl in the front was talking on a cell phone. Were they Mexicans? Could they be Americans? Whatever they were, they were all laughing and having a good time. As they sped off, I could still hear the throbbing bass notes of their music.

I pictured Rico with his brother on this same highway, in an even richer car. Reynaldo was in the car business somehow, as well as cleaning swimming pools. I wondered if Rico was already here. It wasn't like him to be unlucky.

Tucson was nothing like the El Norte I was expecting from TV at Rico's house. The desert city stretched all the way to the mountains with houses that looked Mexican, only much bigger and fancier. I saw a few swimming pools from the highway. I even saw one being cleaned, but I didn't see Rico.

Thoughts of Rico only made me feel worse. For me there was nothing but disappointment and defeat.

As Sandoval drove into a huge compound fenced with chain link and razor wire, I pictured how it might have been different back at the lake. What if I had asked the gabacho for a ride? I might be finding work right now, sending money home soon. He might have taken me all the way to La Perra Flaca.

I would never know.

17

Running out of Time

THE HOLDING ROOM FOR boys was overflowing. Most of us spent the night on the floor. I had my blanket, but I didn't even try to sleep. Partly it was the cold concrete, but mostly it was cold fear. What would they to do to me, and how long would they keep me? A little while, like Miguel, or a long time, like Julio? With Julio, it was four months. If they kept me all summer, with my mother going to Silao every month and returning home with no money, it was all over.

Let them deport me soon, I prayed, so I could somehow try to cross again before the deserts got too hot, before my mother had to sell the goat and the chickens.

Morning came. The boys were all restless and starving. Somebody said they weren't going to feed us with the kids inside until after we were admitted. Food arrived after all. Everybody got a paper sack from McDonald's—egg sandwiches just like the ones at the McDonald's in Silao. I ate every bit and licked the cheese off the wrapper. "Is it like jail, inside?" I asked the boy next to me, who was picking at a scab on his arm. "What did you think?" he said sarcastically. I closed my eyes. I was too low to even get up and move.

I had to wait a long time to be admitted. When my turn came, in the middle of the afternoon, they took my fingerprints. I wouldn't give them my name. A Border Patrol lady named Miller led me down a hallway with many side rooms where kids were being questioned. The gabacha pointed to a bench in the hallway and said, "Take a seat." Her voice was rough, like her pocked face.

"We're too busy to do anything with you," she said, "even to file a plan of return for a juvenile."

I didn't know what she was talking about. I was surprised she spoke such good Spanish.

"There's no room," she said tiredly. "If you complain, then we'll have to take you."

"Take me?"

"Keep you."

If I complained, they would keep me? It didn't make any sense. "How long would you keep me, if I complain?"

"Months, probably. Eventually, you will get an escort back home. You want to complain?"

"No," I said, finally understanding. "Can I go straight to the border instead?"

"That's what I've been trying to tell you. We'll drop you in

Nogales." It looked like the Migra lady hadn't slept either.

"I won't complain," I said.

She looked me in the eye. "You'll go straight home from there?"

"Straight home."

"Good. Go home. Don't try again. Okay?"

I looked at her blankly. She pointed to the door at the far end of the hall, which a guard was holding open. I reached for my backpack and joined two other boys heading that direction.

Outside the door, two buses were waiting. A couple hours later, I was on the border, passing through Nogales, Arizona. We drove by the Wal-Mart.

Above, on the hills, loomed the much larger city of Nogales, Mexico, which I knew all too well. We got out of the bus at the side of the Port of Entry. I followed along as we were led, like cattle, through fence gates and chutes. I was too stunned to think about what to do next. It was early evening, but hot. All that deep snow in the Chiricahua Mountains seemed like I had dreamed it. So too, the journey with Miguel. Being with Julio, that was from another lifetime.

I was numb. I was ashamed. I had failed.

The green shirts had nothing to say. We were walked to one last gate, which was padlocked. It was opened, and we filed through. I watched the gate close behind me, heard the lock click shut. The high metal wall ran as far as I could see. It was a strange feeling, being locked inside your own country.

I had arrived too late for comida at the soup kitchen. I spread out my blanket in the familiar arena of the Plaza de Toros. I missed Julio, who had slept right here. I missed Miguel.

In the morning, I carried sacks for people at the Port of Entry. I made enough to buy an Arizona map. It wasn't nearly as good as Miguel's. It didn't show the dirt roads, the wells and the springs. But it showed the border towns and some of the mountain ranges—the Chiricahuas, but not the Dos Cabezas. It had the interstate highway and it had Willcox. I already knew a lot about Miguel's route. Next time I would follow it all the way to La Perra Flaca. At least I wouldn't run into snowstorms. The problem would be the heat.

The map was from a little store where people bought soda, candy, magazines, and lottery tickets. Every morning, a small tear-off calendar showed the new date. It made me sick every time I went to check. Time and the sun were my enemies. Every day the sun was a little higher in the sky, the streets of Nogales were hotter. I had to get going, but after a week in Nogales, my pesos added up to less than five dollars. I needed bus money east, and food for ten days or two weeks.

April dragged by. By the end of the month it was broiling. I didn't have nearly the money I needed. All I was doing was surviving one day to the next. I'd had six weeks to get ahead of the heat, and I hadn't done it. I thought of Teresa, back home. My sister wouldn't be very proud of me now.

The first of May was unfolding like any other day. During comida in the crowded soup kitchen, as my eyes wandered down the long table, they caught something familiar. On the opposite side, way down near the end, sat a boy with a dirty yellow baseball cap and hair that was blond where it was growing out but dark underneath. For a second I thought it was Rico, but that couldn't be.

I looked again. His nose, the freckles on his cheek . . .

I ate my last bites without blinking, without tasting my food. Rico had left Los Árboles in a yellow Lakers cap.

The boy got up to leave, empty tray in his hand. He was headed in my direction.

My heart jumped out of my chest. "Hey, Rico!" I cried. "How are you? How have you been?"

His eyes landed on me. "Victor! I don't believe it! I don't believe it!"

Outside the parish hall, we fell on each other like we were dying in the desert and had just discovered water. "Am I happy to see you," I said, laughing and crying and embracing my friend.

"Same here, only more so. What in the world are you doing here, Turtle?"

"Crawling north. I thought you were in Tucson, cleaning the swimming pools. Surrounded by beautiful girls."

"I almost got there. I got to Phoenix."

"I made it to Tucson. I saw it from inside a perrera."

Rico looked at me with newfound respect. "I don't believe you, 'mano. You've been to the other side and been deported? Were you trying to find me?"

"I was trying to find work."

"Who gave you the coyote money?"

"Didn't have any. At first I was by myself, then with a kid from Honduras, then with a mojado from Guanajuato traveling on his own. He got caught, then I got caught—it's a long story. What about Fortino and the others you left with? Are they here?"

"We got split up. I've been on my own, too."

Rico's nose was peeling, his lips were chapped, his hands torn up. "You look pretty bad," I said. "All this time, I was sure you had already shook the hand of Mickey Mouse."

"I grabbed him by the tail, and he turned around and bit me."

"How long have you been in Nogales?"

"Six days." Rico pulled a peso coin out of his pocket. "Let's flip."

"What for?"

"To see who tells his story first."

18

Rico won the toss. A block from the soup kitchen, we found a shady spot on the curb and sat down. "Tell me before I start," he said. "Did you talk to my parents, like I asked? Did you tell them what I was doing?"

"I did," I answered cautiously.

"Good. That's all I wanted to know."

"Your mother went to the clinic in Silao that day."

Rico frowned like I'd punched him in the gut. "Victor, what did I just say?"

"Sorry. I thought you would want to know."

"Okay then, I'll start at the beginning. After we left Los Árboles, the five of us went to Guadalajara and caught a first-class bus. Somewhere along the coast—past Los Mochis—my jacket was stolen. A third of my coyote money was in the jacket, five hundred dollars."

"Lots of sharks on those buses, I guess."

"We got off the bus at Sonoyta, on the border with Arizona. A windy, dusty little place. We walked out of town, down an arroyo, past lots of other groups who were waiting. We picked some scrubby trees to sit under and began our own wait.

"Coyotes from three different outfits came to see us. Fortino did all the talking. With the coyotes going back and forth to their bosses, there was a lot of waiting. Part of why it took so long was because we didn't have as much money as were supposed to."

"Because of your jacket being stolen?"

"None of us had the full fifteen hundred. The coyotes wanted telephone numbers on the other side, people who would guarantee the rest. Nobody gave a name or a number. Fortino said that all sorts of horrible things might happen to your friends or relatives if they couldn't pay. Finally, Fortino got a coyote to agree to a thousand apiece. Five hundred up front, five hundred when we made it to Tucson."

"Sounds like you got a good deal."

"We thought so. We figured we had just saved five hundred dollars apiece. We walked east a couple of miles to meet our driver, within sight of the new fence the Americans built to keep the coyotes from driving into a huge cactus park."

"They built a metal wall like here in Nogales?"

"It's all different. Every four feet, there's a heavy iron post in the ground, with railroad ties welded across. The fence is only five feet high. It's to keep vehicles out, but let the wildlife go back and forth.

That's what we heard."

"You climbed over it?"

"Went all the way around it. Our driver was no older than me. The other guy up front was the pollero who was going to walk us across the desert. The truck looked awful and sounded worse. There was already a group from Guerrero in the back. Eleven of them and five of us made sixteen. The bumper scraped whenever we crossed a gully.

"We drove a couple of hours east to where the cactus park ended. From there, the border is just a barbed wire fence, and it's Indian land on the other side. The driver and the pollero bent over a steel fencepost that somebody had already weakened with a hacksaw. We crossed the wire, barely creeping, headlights off. The driver leaned his head out to find his way around the bushes and gullies. After about fifteen minutes we got to a dirt road, and he turned the headlights on. We started to breathe easier, but not really. There was no shell over the back of the truck. We were eating dust the whole way.

"The road got better and we started going forty or fifty. Out the back, we saw some lights. There was a vehicle coming up behind us."

"Border Patrol?"

"That's what we thought. They came on really fast. I mean *really* fast. Our driver tried to accelerate, but we were heavy and the motor was a piece of junk. Whatever was chasing us was new and powerful. In no time at all, it was on us. I mean, twenty feet behind. Their high beams blinded us so bad, we couldn't see what it was. Suddenly they turned on a row of even brighter lights across the top of their cab. I made out a guy's arm sticking out the passenger window with a pistol. He was yelling at us to stop. We went around a little corner. I could finally see what was chasing us—a black pickup, a new Dodge Ram. Two guys standing behind the cab had automatic weapons pointed right at us. They started spraying bullets—*rat-a-tat-tat*. I was sure I was dead."

"People got killed?"

"No, they were shooting just over our heads. That got the attention of our driver. He finally stopped, and for a couple of seconds, everything was quiet as the grave. The two men in the cab of the Dodge got out. No uniforms—we had no idea who they were and what this was all about. One had that pistol, the other a short assault rifle. They ordered our driver and pollero to get out with their hands up. The pistolero started shouting at our driver, accusing him of smuggling, and then he pistol-whipped him. The other guy punched our pollero hard in the stomach. In the back of the truck, everybody was whispering. I heard the leader of the men from Guerrero say it was the Federal Judicial Police. The way he said 'Judiciales,' it scared me to death."

"They were Mexican police, and they chased you into the States?"

"Ten minutes north of the border, at least."

"But why?"

"The crossing is supposed to cost fifteen hundred dollars, remember? Guess what—when we only paid a thousand, the

Judiciales didn't get their bribe. Our cut-rate coyote must have thought that the police weren't keeping close track of all the groups waiting outside of town. I found out later we should have stayed in a safe house, in Sonoyta. If you're staying in one, it means you're safe from the police—they've been paid."

Rico picked up a rock and threw it at a pigeon. He missed.

"How'd you get away? Where are the others?"

"I'm getting there. The Judiciales made us drive back toward the border. They stayed right behind us with those blinding lights on. They made our pollero ride with them. Their pistolero was in the cab of our truck with his gun to the driver's head. In the back of the truck, people were whispering about how everybody's money would be stolen by the police, about prison, about torture. Someone said everybody should jump out of the truck as soon as we reached rough ground. 'They got two AK-47s and a mini,' the leader from Guerrero said. 'They'll mow you down.'"

"I would have died of fright."

"I asked Fortino if it was true, about jail and all the rest. 'Say your prayers,' he whispered. All I knew was, I had to get away. I squeezed toward the edge of the pickup. We were going around a curve. I went flying, right into a narrow spot between two bushes."

"Did they shoot?"

"The shots went right over my head. I kind of tumbled when I hit the ground, and was out of their lights. I ran like I've never run before. Tripping, falling down, running, tripping, running, running . . ."

"What about the others?"

"Who knows? I still don't know if they went to jail, or what. Probably they did. I never saw them in Sonoyta. I hiked all the way back there the next night."

"Why would you go back there?"

"Our coyote had half of my money. They're supposed to get you to where you're going, as many tries as it takes."

"You still had the other five hundred?"

"Still had it. I waited three days until they had more pollos ready to go—a group from Oaxaca with women and kids. This time they let us off on the highway to Tijuana, along the border with some kind of wildlife refuge. We walked north for four days. Fortunately, it wasn't that hot yet, but even so we ran out of water. Only half of us made it. You had to be really strong."

"What happened to the other half?"

"When they couldn't keep up, they got left behind."

"Abandoned?"

"The chicken wranglers don't care. They get paid by the head. They still make good money if only half make it, that's what I heard."

"They left women and children behind in the desert?"

"Including a woman from Chicago who said she was the aunt of the boy and girl who were with her. They were eight and nine, and didn't look a thing like her. Later on, when she caught up, without the kids, she told us she was hired to go get the kids way down in Mexico and bring them across. Take them to their parents in Pennsylvania."

"She abandoned the boy and the girl? What happened to them?"

"Who knows? Our pollero said that the Border Patrol's search-and-rescue helicopters would pick them up."

"But what if they were never found?"

"I try not to think about that. There was nothing I could do. They never would have made it through the Growler Mountains. It was rough. We hid outside a town called Ajo. The American coyotes showed up late the next day. We drove past a cemetery for people who died in the crossing. All these small white crosses with no names, just the words NO OLVIDADO."

"*Not forgotten.* What's that supposed to mean, if nobody knows who they were?"

"I'm only telling you what I saw. They took us to a safe house in Phoenix. I waited two weeks for a ride to a safe house in Tucson. They were messing with me, trying to get a name, a phone number—more money. The ride was supposed to be coming any minute, but then we got raided by the Border Patrol. They didn't have any room in the juvenile detention center, so here I am."

"How much money do you have left?"

"Less than a hundred. Those American coyotes got three hundred out of me in Phoenix. What do you have?"

"Thirteen dollars' worth of pesos if I'm lucky. If you go back to Sonoyta, will your coyote give you another try?"

"After I paid on the other end, why would he? I'm in a bad way, 'mano. Now, tell me about your own disasters."

19

Spiders in a Can

I T WAS EVENING AND starting to cool down by the time I finished my own story. "Let's find something to eat," Rico said. "I've never been so hungry in my life."

"I can wait until the soup kitchen tomorrow," I said.

"Tell me this. What is the one food you would die for, right now?"

"Chocolate-covered frozen banana on a stick."

Rico pointed to an ice-cream cart down the street. He pulled some pesos out of his pocket. "My treat, to celebrate. Let's see if they have those."

They did. We stood in the shade of a plaster wall to keep the chocolate from melting. Rico gobbled his up but I went slow, enjoying every bite. The chocolate reminded me of my last night at home. "I just realized this," I said. "You don't have a backpack."

"I lost it yesterday. I have to get another one, and some clothes. Mine stink."

As I finished and was licking my fingers, two cholos approached, flashing some sort of signs. They sported white muscle shirts, baggy pants, flashy sneakers. We talked a little, and then the one with no hair except a rattail said, "We can get you though the tunnels."

"No, thanks," Rico said. "Once was enough."

Grinning, the cholos shambled off. "What was that about?" I asked. Before, when I had told him about Julio floating through on an inner tube, me staying behind, he hadn't said a thing about having tried the tunnels himself.

"It's how I lost my backpack," Rico replied sheepishly.

"When was this?"

"Just yesterday. I met a cholo—Nardo was his name. For a hundred dollars, he said he'd take me through. It sounded like a deal. Let me tell you, it was creepy in there. It's really long, smells bad, and it's pitch dark. Traffic rumbling over your head, side tunnels, people appearing and disappearing like ghosts. Lots of cholos live in there, huffing spray. Nardo's flashlight was a piece of junk. Finally I saw the faint light at the other end, reflections of streetlights. When we got close, there was a heavy chain-link gate across the entrance—like you were talking about, like you were afraid of floating into on the inner tube."

"How did you lose your backpack?"

"The cholos took it, and the hundred dollars in my pocket. A bunch of them came out of the side tunnels with sticks and knives, like a pack of hyenas, only worse. Nardo laughed and called me a fool. I would have lost my last hundred if they'd stripped me, like they were talking about. They let me go, laughing at me all the way back."

"Well, you survived."

"What a fool I was. I can't tell you how good it felt to see you, Turtle, after everything I've been through."

"Will you keep trying to cross?"

"Of course. Everything will be fine once I get to my brother's. Now we can team up and figure out how to get across this stupid border once and for all. Maybe my brother will put both of us to work."

"Right now that sounds too good to be true."

At the Plaza de Toros, we spread out my blanket and my map of Arizona, which included Mexico for a hundred miles south. I tried to talk him into Miguel's route, all the way to La Perra Flaca.

Rico went from looking sour to shaking his head. "Too far, too many chances to get caught. Plus, that was March and this is May. The water you found would have dried up by now."

"About that, you might be right," I had to admit.

Rico pointed to the huge Tohono O'odham reservation. "Everyone says this is where most people are crossing. The Indians have seventy or eighty miles of the border. Maybe it's not patrolled very much."

We took a closer look at the map. A paved road ran east and west through the middle of the reservation. At a town called Sells, the pavement dipped within thirty miles of the border. "We hike to that road," Rico said. "From there, Tucson is only an hour's drive."

"When we get to the road, who's going to give us a ride?"

"The Indians, I guess."

"The Indians have cars?"

"In the States, who doesn't?"

I didn't like the uncertainty, but had to wonder if Miguel might think this was worth trying, now that it was May. The shorter the distance, the better our chances of surviving the desert. I would let Rico decide. It was his money that was going to buy the bus tickets and the supplies.

In the morning, we found a shop with cheap used clothing. My old T-shirts and underwear went in the trash. Rico wasn't the only one who smelled bad. Rico found a backpack, and we both found better sneakers. At the bus terminal, Rico bought two tickets for Altar, a town a couple hours to the southwest.

The bus rolled up the hills and out of Nogales, onto the desert plains sprinkled with those huge factories, the maquiladoras. Soon we saw only skinny cows, cactus, and mesquite. I hoped to God I had seen the last of Nogales.

At Altar we got out our map and compared it with the one posted inside the bus station. We had a decision to make. Mexico had border towns near both ends of the reservation—Sonoyta to the west, Sasabe to the east. Rico said he'd had enough of Sonoyta, and Sasabe was closer to the Indian land.

The only problem was, there was no bus to Sasabe. We turned from the ticket window and started asking questions. There were plenty of mojados to ask. You go to Sasabe by van or truck, a guy told us. Go to the plaza, you'll see.

The town was flooded with wets. The park inside the plaza was overflowing with them, and with polleros. Rico and I hadn't even found a place to sit down when we began to hear their pitches. "Florida, Los Angeles, Chi-cago—wherever you want to go . . . Three thousand dollars to Boston with a job guaranteed as a dishwasher." Five times in ten minutes, we were asked if we were looking for guides.

The plaza was ringed with parked vans. Many had their back doors flung open and were selling jugs of water. Most had a sign in the window. We went to have a closer look. The signs said SASABE.

Three, four times, we asked about the cost of the ride to Sasabe. "Who are you with?" they would ask back. "We're by ourselves," we would say. "No room," they would tell us. Try to push it, and they told us to go away.

We were halfway around the plaza before we got an explanation. "If you two are by yourselves," a driver told us, "forget about it."

"Why is that?" I asked.

"Crossing on your own, that's bad for business."

"Whose business?"

"The coyotes, who do you think? They don't like people trying to cross on their own. They'll charge you five hundred dollars apiece if they catch you trying."

"What for?"

"They make you pay them so that nobody will mess with you— understand? Don't waste my time. Go home if you have any sense."

We stepped aside. "Protection money," Rico fumed. "Did your Miguel ever tell you about that part of trying it on your own?"

"He never mentioned it."

"I think we have a problem."

"We'll stay out of their way," I said. I didn't let on, but my confidence was shaken. "Let's keep looking."

At last we found someone who liked the green color of Rico's money. "Ten dollars apiece to Sasabe, and there might be room. Be back in an hour. Buy your supplies in Altar. Sasabe is a chicken-scratch town."

At Altar's biggest grocery, Super El Coyote, we bought our supplies: food for a five-day hike across the Indian reservation, water, cheap sunglasses, a pocketknife, and needle-nose pliers. All the money that remained was a few dollars of Rico's, in pesos.

We hurried back and got packed with thirteen men into a Suburban with the seats taken out. The others were from Michoacán, wets like us, but with coyote money. They were going to meet their pollero in Sasabe.

The road north was mostly unpaved, with heavy traffic. The driver kept the windows up to keep out the dust. I thought I was going to suffocate. We were all tangled up in there like a nest of spiders in a tin can, and the air-conditioning was broken. Rico made a joke about the Suburbans being put together in Silao. He said his sister's husband was to blame.

I didn't have the breath to grunt a reply. At least we were moving, and the direction was north.

20

Sitting Here in Limbo

SASABE, AT LAST. Finally, the doors opened and the spiders crawled out of the can. The men from Michoacán took off to find their pollero. Rico and I stood there on unsteady feet with no particular place to go. A dust devil whirled sand and trash down the street and threw it into our faces.

The noise of the small desert town made up for its size, with honking horns, barking dogs, a policeman blowing a whistle, firecrackers going *pop-pop-pop*. The streets were hot as lava, but even so they were packed with hundreds and hundreds of mojados making their last preparations or killing time. The only shade, under a few spindly cottonwoods, was all taken.

From the end of the street, we could see the border. Trucks were backed up there, waiting to have their produce inspected for stowaways. Beyond the Port of Entry, the gas stations, convenience stores, and fast food places of Sasabe, Arizona, shimmered in the heat. So did a mountain range, spiny as an iguana's back, looming above to the north and west. One peak in the middle, with square, tapering sides like a monument, stood much higher than all the rest.

"Those mountains are in the States," I said. "We could get into them on foot from here."

Rico made a face. "Those mountains would spit us out like a hairball."

I pulled out the map of Arizona. Baboquivari was the name of the range. The Baboquivari Mountains rose on the border and ran north. Their crest was the eastern boundary of the Tohono O'odham Indian reservation. I was studying the map hard, like Miguel would have. The tower mountain was called Baboquivari Peak. It soared more than a mile above the desert floor.

Rico was frowning. He could see where I was looking. "There has to be a dirt road on the Mexican side that goes around those mountains. All we need is one more ride, so we can cross into the Indian land where the hiking won't be straight up and down."

"I guess you're right," I said.

How to come by that last ride, that was the problem. There were plenty of vans and pickups to be seen leaving along a dirt road heading west toward the Indian reservation. But those vehicles were full of mojados who had scraped together the big money.

We told each other there had to be people who lived in that direction, in ranchos too small to appear on the map. Some of them must come to Sasabe for food and supplies.

We found several such people. It was easy to see they didn't want to waste their time with us. They would barely admit that they lived out of town. As soon as we brought up needing a ride, they shook us off quick.

It was hot, and our backpacks were heavy. Rico was red in the face and murmuring about the heat, the money being gone, and the trouble we were in.

"Something will come along," I said. "We'll start walking from here if we have to."

"Too far, Turtle. We'd go through all our water before we even crossed the wire."

Rico took out his frustration at a video arcade, on an army of green-shirted soldiers who blew up like squashes and bled rivers when you blasted them with your AK-47.

The machine ate peso coins like candy, but what could I say? It was Rico's money.

Ten minutes later, along came a bare-chested punk three or four years older than us. I was shocked by the tattoo on his chest, a gory Christ with barbed wire for a crown of thorns and much dripping blood.

For whatever reason, the punk had his sights on us. He had a rockero haircut, short all around except for a purple forelock that hung down nearly to the top of his nose. Apparently he didn't know how stupid it looked, especially when he flicked it back, which he did as a habit. It was like the switching tail of a donkey stuck on his forehead.

"What are you guys up to?" he said as he lit a cigarette. Money was written all over him: silver nylon pants, snakeskin boots, gold chains around his neck, diamond studs in his ears.

"Sitting here in limbo," Rico replied with a shrug.

"Jimmy Cliff song! You like reggae, Bob Marley?"

"Who doesn't?"

"Right on, 'mano. 'Stand up for your rights.' What else do you like? Rap, metal, punk, pop? What kind of CDs you got in your backpack?"

"I lost my CDs and my player in Nogales."

"Don't tell me about Nogales. I'm *from* Nogales. These days, I wouldn't give you spit for it. Same goes for Juárez and Tijuana. So many Migra, they sit with their trucks in view of each other, waiting to pounce."

"You can't even use the tunnels in Nogales anymore," Rico said.

"Tell me about it." The punk flashed a tattoo on his wrist at us. It was familiar, a triangle of blue dots.

"What does that mean?" I asked.

"Don't you know anything? Barrio Libre, from Nogales! I've done it all . . . I've been a cholo, a ratero, and a bajadero, but I have graduated."

"Now you're a pollero?"

"Polleros and coyotes are what you call us. We call ourselves gangsters."

"Gangsters?"

He pretended he was firing a submachine gun. "Like the Mafia.

146

My name is Jarra. Tony Jarra, but you can call me the Mosquito."

The Mosquito put his cigarette out on a caterpillar that was crawling across the video machine. It made a putrid smell. "Obviously, you guys are trying to go north to make some money," Jarra said. "How much do you expect to make on the other side?"

"Six dollars an hour," I said.

"Doing what?" He threw back his head to make his donkey tail swing.

"Field work."

Jarra spat at the caterpillar, which was still squirming. "Some kind of Pancho Villa you are. How about you, Blondie," he said to Rico. "Hoe the weeds also, pick the lettuce?"

"Clean the swimming pools."

"Aaah . . ." the gangster said, breathing out a long plume of smoke. "The swimming pools of the rich. A real Zapata, you are."

"What about you, Mosquito?" Rico kidded. "What kind of revolutionary are you?"

"Where have you been? Even the stupid ranchera ballads glorify us these days. We are heroes to the mojados and their families back home, while making fools of the Border Patrol. Aside from all that, there is the money. As a guide, I am paid one hundred dollars for every pollo I get to the pick-up point. How does a thousand dollars a week sound to you?"

"It sounds like a lot of money," Rico said.

"Party, party, party! Back when I was a mule, I made eight hundred dollars a trip, three trips a month. You two have strong backs.

You could start out carrying, learn the trails as mules, then graduate to guiding, like I did."

"Only one problem," I said. "If we get caught running drugs, we rot in jail."

"You'll rot in Sasabe instead. It's going to be a warm summer. Think about it."

The gangster slouched on by.

Rico had his head down, as if deep in thought. Then he slammed his fist on the video machine. "Let's get out of here," he said.

We followed a dry creek out of town, toward a mesquite thicket where new arrivals congregated and slept. All the while, I could tell Rico was getting worked up. Suddenly he stopped in his tracks and said, "I blame my father for this."

"How? Why?"

"Think about all those years when it would have been so easy."

"What would have been so easy?"

"To move his family to the States. I could have grown up there, and not have to go through all of this. He knew better! Too stubborn, that's all!"

I pointed to a mesquite that would be easy to crawl under. Nobody had taken it. "Let's get out of the sun for a while, Rico. The heat is getting to you."

"You fight off the rattlesnakes. I'm going back into town."

Just the thought of rattlesnakes made my throat tighten and my skin crawl. "You don't need to scare me, Rico. I'm scared enough, just like you. I tell you, everything will be better."

"When?"

"Tonight, tomorrow."

"I'm not so sure," he said. "I'm going back into town. I'll see you later if the snakes haven't gotten you."

"I'll be here," I said.

It was getting dark, the first hint of a breeze beginning to arrive, when Rico finally returned. He looked better. "You eaten anything?" I asked.

"I'm starving, but I got our problems taken care of."

"Here, have a cheese stick. You found us a ride?"

"Better than that. I got us covered all the way to Tucson, to my brother's."

"What are you talking about? How is that possible?"

"I called him up."

"Reynaldo?"

"Isn't that what I just said?"

"I thought you didn't have a phone number."

Rico reached for a package of tortillas. Before I could say anything, he tore it open at the wrong end, opposite the plastic zipper. We wouldn't be able to reseal it.

Rico hadn't noticed. "Here," he said, giving me a tortilla, chewing on another. "The phone number was supposed to be a last resort. I wasn't going to use it until I got to Tucson. Well, now is what I would call a last resort. I reached him. It wasn't easy, and he wasn't happy about everything that's happened, but he wasn't surprised.

The important thing is, he vouched for us with Jarra's coyote."

"Who's that?"

"I don't know his real name. He calls himself The Venom."

"What kind of person would call himself The Venom? You met the actual coyote, the head man?"

"Through Jarra, then some other guy."

"Where did you have this conference and do the phone calling?"

"Jarra's motel room. What difference does it make?"

"What have you done, Rico? I thought we were going on our own!"

"It wasn't going to work! Isn't that obvious?"

"How would we know unless we tried?"

"Calm down, Victor. You'll see. We need the protection of a group, and my brother is willing to cover us."

"Did he say anything about a job for me?"

"We didn't discuss it."

"Without a job, how will I pay him back?"

"He wasn't worrying about it. Why should you?"

"Have you forgotten? I have to send my money to my family."

"Paying back Reynaldo is the least of our troubles. First we have to get there, and I've taken care of that. You should be happy."

"I'm not."

"I'll pay back your coyote money myself."

"I couldn't let you do that."

"Try and stop me. Now shut up and eat. We're leaving in half an hour."

21

Your Name Is Liar

"WHERE ARE THE OTHERS?" I asked as Rico and I climbed into the back of a coyote van. The seats had been removed. The van had an Arizona plate.

Jarra gave me a scornful look. "The others? That's nothing you need to know."

In the back of the van were two large backpacks overflowing with packages of tortillas and canned goods, mostly meat and fish. We sat on a big cooler with no ice that was filled with gallon jugs of water. "You might have been wondering why I didn't invite one of you to sit up front in the passenger seat," Jarra called as he drove out of Sasabe. "My friend is sitting next to me."

"Who is your friend?" Rico asked.

Jarra reached over and picked something up off the seat—a big pistol in a holster. "Recognize it?"

"Should we?"

"Border Patrol gun—forty-caliber Beretta, semiautomatic. Eleven rounds in the magazine. Reloads in a heartbeat."

The Mosquito put the gun down and reached for a CD. He turned the volume high as it would go—some punk like himself rapping about the Border Patrol committing crimes against innocent mojados. Jarra rapped along as he fishtailed around the curves on the washboard road, leaving behind a rooster tail of dust. "Hang on," Rico said. We had to brace to keep from falling to the floor.

I told myself to remember that millions of wets, including Rico's father and mine, had been at the mercy of coyotes. Still, it was impossible not to loathe Jarra. For such a vile person to sport El Cristo Rey on his chest, this was a terrible sin.

For the time being, I didn't have to look at his tattoos. Our driver was wearing a tan soccer jersey to blend in with the desert. His stupid purple forelock was sticking out from above the strap on a green baseball cap worn backward. Gone were the gold chains around his neck, the diamond studs in his ears. The chicken wrangler wanted to blend in with his chickens, in case he got caught.

"There's room for another fifteen or twenty mojados in here," I joked to Rico. "What's the deal? Seriously, why just us?"

"Who knows?" he grunted. Rico was looking very unhappy.

"I guess we'll pick some up along the way to our starting point," I said. "Why all this food and water? We didn't have to supply our own?"

Rico didn't bother to answer. If he was annoyed, how was I to feel? He'd called his brother without even bringing it up, arranged all of this in my name without ever including me. And then there was the fifteen hundred dollars hanging over my head. Easy for him, but how was I going to repay it?

I turned my attention to the rugged Baboquivari Mountains rising sharply from the desert plain. We skirted the foot of them and continued west, in and out of many gullies, on the Mexican side of the Indian reservation. The road had a lot of traffic for an area so thinly settled. We hadn't yet laid eyes on a rancho.

Jarra must have been bored. Suddenly he turned the music down. "Hey, Villa," he called, meaning me. "Zapata told me you thought you two could cross the border all by yourselves. Hike through the desert, just the two of you."

"I thought we could," I admitted.

"That's crazy, Villa. Especially in the Death Season."

"What's that, Mosquito?"

"If you have to ask, you wouldn't have lasted two days. Death Season is May until October. Have you checked the calendar lately?"

The Mosquito started laughing, then said, "We'll find out soon enough what you're made of, Villa. Zapata said you could handle it. I'm not so sure."

"Victor Flores is my name."

"You are a runt, Villa. With a name like flowers, I think you are also too weak."

"Who cares what you think," I said, "as long as you get me through."

Jarra bristled. "You ought to show some respect. I don't like your attitude."

Shut up and drive, I wanted to say. Suddenly, Jarra was slowing. He seemed to be looking for a turnoff. We had passed many dirt tracks heading north, toward the border, but he was looking south, which made no sense.

Jarra did turn left, to the south, onto a road so rough he had to go into four-wheel drive. The road wound through the brush like a sidewinder. I guessed we were about to pick up a group of mojados who had been stashed where there was shelter and water. We parked with the engine off and waited for half an hour. To the north and west, the sun was going down fast, starting to flatten above the horizon.

The sun had just set when we heard the drone of an airplane. It seemed to be getting closer and closer. Through the brush, we caught a glimpse of a small white single-engine plane it as it came in for a landing. An emergency landing, I thought. There was no airport here, no airstrip.

I was wrong. Jarra fired up the motor and we rolled ahead. Another couple of gullies, and the airstrip was right in front of us. It was rough, crudely hacked out of the cactus and mesquite. The plane had landed safely.

"Are you going to fly us to Tucson?" I joked to Jarra.

"Time to make yourself useful," he snarled, driving right up to the airplane.

I looked at Rico, but he didn't have any answers. We rolled back the side door of the van and got out as Jarra threw open the back. His pistol was stuck under his belt. "How many?" Jarra yelled at the pilot, who had moved to the back of the plane and opened the side door.

"Thirteen, as arranged," the potbellied pilot yelled back. He was sweating, and he looked nervous. "Let's go, I want to get out of here." He stooped to lift a heavy package down to Jarra. It was bigger than a bag of cement and entirely wrapped in brown plastic packing tape.

"Hey, you two," Jarra yelled at us. "I hand them to you, you pack them in the back of the van. Hurry up!"

By this time I had figured out why the pilot was so nervous, and in such a hurry. "Drugs," I whispered to Rico.

"Just do what he says," Rico said from the side of his mouth.

Jarra flicked his donkey tail. "Hurry! Help me with these bales."

I was about to say no, and see what would happen. "Don't do anything stupid," Rico said. "He'll shoot you."

"One thousand and forty pounds of prime mota," Jarra crowed as we drove off a few minutes later. The plane was already airborne. Jarra started playing a CD really loud, and pounding on the steering wheel.

"Where's he going with this marijuana?" I asked Rico quietly.

"No idea," Rico said.

"You think he's going to drop it off, then take us to meet our group?"

Rico shook his head, whatever that meant.

Jarra turned the sound down. "What's up with you mules back there?"

"I'm no mule," I said, but suddenly everything came into focus. I gave Rico a hard look, which he ignored.

"Remember, Jarra," Rico said, "we're only carrying food or water."

Jarra turned around and grinned like a smiling dog. "Oh, excuse me, I forgot. What difference does it make?"

Jarra turned the music up again. I glared at Rico. "What's going on? Come on, tell me. Didn't you say Reynaldo put up the money?"

"I told you before, I never had his phone number."

"You lied to me?"

"It was for your own good. We work off what we owe. One trip, that's all we have to make. They wanted us to make two, but I made them agree to one. And we don't have to carry the drugs."

"As if that will make any difference if we get caught helping drug smugglers? We'll go to prison, maybe for the rest of our lives. Idiot, what were you thinking?"

"I thought my name was Rico."

"It's Liar," I said. "Your name is Liar. How could you do this to me? To my family? You've betrayed me."

"Settle down. It's for your own good. We didn't stand a chance in the desert, just the two of us. How were we going to find water, tell me that? They know where the water is. They'll have transportation for us all the way to Tucson. How were we going to get to Tucson?"

"You said we were going to take our chances catching a ride. With the Indians—remember?"

"Well, I got us a ride. So, settle down. We were in a desperate situation. If I told you, you wouldn't have gone along."

"You're right about that."

"You'll thank me later."

"I'll thank you right now. Thanks for nothing, 'mano."

I had nothing more to say to him. I was angrier than I'd been in my whole life. Furious.

I thought about bailing out of the van, into the darkness, but my backpack was out of reach and Jarra was watching me closely in the mirror. If I got away without him shooting me down, what then? Even if I made it back to Sasabe, how was I going to start over and cross the border? Rico knew all of this, knew I'd have to stick with him.

I was so upset, I hadn't been following the twists and turns the van was taking in the dark, with no headlights. We'd been climbing, gradually, and the rocks had been getting bigger. At the last, Jarra drove into an enclosure of gigantic boulders, like a bandit hideaway, which is what it turned out to be. Two other vehicles were parked there, with shadowy figures milling around behind the glow of cigarettes. As soon as we drove in, they started unloading the bales from the back of our van.

The mules looked rough, like the hardened criminals they no doubt were. They used bungee cords to attach the drug bales to wooden packframes with canvas shoulder straps. Those two huge backpacks we were supposed to carry, stuffed full of food, felt like they were loaded with rocks. I jammed my pocketknife and pliers in an outside pocket. Our own backpacks with food, water, and clothes were going to be left behind.

The mules were saddling up. We did the same. I could barely lift my pack to my knee and swing it onto my shoulders. I staggered, but I stood. Everybody bent to pick up a gallon jug of water. Rico and I did the same. A man with a scar through his mustache came over and told us he was the boss. "Morales is my name," he said. "I don't know you from anybody, but we lost a couple of men. What is this about you carrying only food?"

Rico got us into this. He was going to have to do the explaining. "Jarra promised," Rico said lamely.

Morales spat on Rico's shoes. "What are you, Migra informers, or simply fools?"

"Fools," Rico said.

Morales showed his teeth and laughed. "For now, you fools can carry the food. Those packs are at least as heavy as a bale of mota. I'm going to be watching you two very carefully. Don't mess with me, or you won't live to regret it."

"Wonderful," I said, when Morales was at a safe distance. Rico wasn't saying a thing.

The mule train started out under a brilliant full moon. It numbered seventeen: thirteen carrying the mota, two of us carrying the food, and two gangsters with light backpacks. Unlike the polleros who smuggled people, the drug smugglers were armed. Morales walked in front with an assault rifle. It had one of those big, curving ammunition clips. No doubt he had extra clips in his backpack. Jarra, taking up the rear, had that semiautomatic handgun at his hip.

The pace was brutal, the weight on my back crushing. The route wound among car-sized boulders, always uphill. The night was hot. I was breathing hard and dripping with sweat.

It took less than an hour to reach the border. It felt like an eternity. We passed the packs across, then crawled underneath. Only four strands here. Morales and Jarra disguised our tracks on both sides of the fence.

We saddled up and started into Arizona. Once again, I had crossed the wire.

22

I DIDN'T KNOW IF I HAD the strength. I had to lean into the climb, dig in with every step, push off with everything in my legs. The night air was steaming. I was breathing hard. The sweat dripped into my eyes and stung. In the moonlight, giant cactus looked like tortured humans, arms twisted up and down. Some stood tall as telephone poles. Everything looked dreamlike, but this was no dream. I had become a mule.

Whether Rico was in front of me or behind, I had no idea. I was staying away from him. It was anger that got me through those first miles, along with hurt, disbelief, and disillusionment. How could he have deceived me like that?

My lungs were on fire. I thought my heart would explode. The gallon of water in my hand felt heavy as an adobe brick. By the time we stopped to rest, I'd never been so thirsty in my life. I took only a few sips. There was no telling how long my gallon would have to last. I bent over double to try to get the weight off my shoulders, if only for a few seconds. None of the mules were asking how far we were going or when we might get there. We were only pack animals.

Two minutes, and Morales was yelling, "Let's get going!"

I told myself to be on the lookout for the Border Patrol. I had to be ready to drop my pack and run. But as the smuggler's trail continued up and down the flanks of the mountains, winding among boulders, thorny trees, and endless cactus, I had to keep up with the mule in front of me and couldn't afford any looking around. My eyes stayed on the rocky footing and the thorny scrub punishing my hands and arms. Everything that grew bristled with needles and claws, and reached out to draw blood.

The punishment went on all night. The moon had nearly crossed the sky by the time we were finally told to take off our packs. Rico dropped his next to mine. "Look, turtle," he said.

"Don't call me Turtle," I growled, and took a swig of water. I was down to half.

He pointed. "No, look at the turtle."

Twenty feet away, a tortoise was crawling into its burrow. I looked at it. I didn't say a thing.

The first light rimmed the ridge at our backs. The desert was dead still, as if holding its breath before an explosion. I saw a tarantula making haste, a scorpion disappearing under a rock. One thing was for sure: When the sun came up, we were going to fry.

The boss came over and told us to break out the food. "One tin of meat for everybody," Morales ordered. "Two tortillas."

My back was so stiff I could barely move. Rico got to his feet. He started pulling food out of my pack instead of his. It took me a second to realize he was doing me a favor. "These packs would break the back of a mule with four legs," he said.

I didn't bother to reply.

Rico passed out the food. The meat was jellied ham. I broke off small pieces and ate them slowly, with the tortillas. I licked my fingers for the salt and the grease. As dawn spread a soft orange glow across the desert floor below, the stillness came to a sudden end. Every bird in the desert, it seemed, began to sing at the same time. I took out the pliers and began to pull cactus needles from my arms, hands, and ankles. The pliers were soon making the rounds of the other mules. I never saw them again.

The mules were pointing at something—a herd of wild pigs, a stone's throw away. Unbelievably, they were taking bites out of the prickly pear cactus. I thought of my sisters, all the work they would do with those cactus pads to make nopales. Jarra aimed his forefinger and thumb, squeezed, yelled, "Die!" The wild pigs took off in a clatter.

As the light came up, we could see a grid of rusty red roads running east and west through the flats of the reservation below. White specks were raising dust on those roads—Border Patrol, Jarra announced, as if we didn't know. "They catch people like flies down there."

The oldest mule, who had a receding hairline and a perpetual grin carved in the lines of his face, pointed at a shiny, stationary disc in the western sky. "Hey, Mosquito," he said. "What is that thing? Spaceship? Mojados from space?"

"Don't you know anything, Paco? That's Fat Albert, the Migra blimp. Don't worry, the scum who live inside can't see us way over here. They've never put a blimp over these mountains. They think there is nothing to see."

"Why is that, Mosquito?"

"Too rugged for lazy Mexicans, that's what they think. They are fools! Even their helicopter patrols are useless here. Where we go, there is so much cover, they have as much chance of finding Osama bin Laden."

The mules all found this very funny.

"What about those new drones, Mosquito?" Paco asked with pretended seriousness. "The ones that fly high, with no pilot?"

"They don't work, either. Even their infrared cameras can't see us because of all the rocks. The rocks give off heat, same as we do."

"I think the Mosquito, like Fat Albert, is full of hot gas," Paco said. "Nobody light a match."

Once again, the mules had a good laugh. This time, Jarra was offended. "You guys need to learn some respect," he said, and put his hand on his Beretta.

It got very quiet. Even Paco's grin disappeared. Evidently the mules believed that the Mosquito was crazy enough to start shooting.

Morales spat, then grabbed up his assault rifle. "Let's get moving.

We have a long way to go. I'm warning everyone. If you fall behind today, you will die."

I cringed. I had been sure we were going to hide from the sun, like the desert animals.

As we got going, a dawn breeze touched my face, but the coolness was gone as soon as it arrived. The sun rose and shot into the sky. Before long it was beating on us like a hammer. The earth was on fire, and so was I.

It wasn't long before my cheeks were burning, my ears and my eyelids, too. My lips began to crack, my tongue to thicken. Swallowing became very difficult. The water in my jug was hot as tea from the stove. I drank it, careful not to spill a drop. My body was spilling enough. My scalp was drenched with sweat. So were my armpits, my neck, and my arms. Suddenly—I couldn't tell why—I stopped sweating. I started licking my lips to keep them from splitting. It made them worse.

I was getting dizzy, and I began to stumble. I had a rash on my arms and a bad headache. My fingers were swollen. Through my sneakers, the ground felt like volcano lava. My tongue was swollen. My thirst was unbearable. I had no spit in my mouth, only a thick dry paste.

I had been saving the last few gulps of water. I needed them. I drank every drop.

I had to get away, go somewhere in my mind. I went home to Los Árboles, to the sweet mountain air of home. I had the hoe in my hands and was weeding. The corn was already six inches high.

There was moisture in the air.

Suddenly I could hear the rain. I could hear it distinctly. I was in the house, in my room with Chuy. We were lying on our backs listening to the night rain as the lightning cracked above El Cubilete and thunder rolled and rumbled through the mountains. We could hear the water rushing down the gutters and filling up the rain barrels. "Victor, don't go," Chuy was pleading. "You know I'm afraid of the lightning." "It's okay," I kept telling him. "You're a big boy now."

I found myself stopped in my tracks. The mule train had come to a standstill. Someone ahead had stumbled and fallen. The mule was trying to rise under his eighty pounds of mota. He fell again. Someone finally pulled him to his feet. His knee was bleeding. I felt a sensation that didn't make any sense. My skin was getting cooler instead of hotter. No mistake, I was cooler all over. I raked my forearm. It was dry and flaky as an old snakeskin. When I blinked, my eyelids scraped. My body was going haywire. The heat was going to kill me.

We started up again. The next to fall was the mule in front of me. Somehow I found the strength to pull him to his feet. Morales let everybody rest. The mule I had helped, young and not so tough-looking, turned and thanked me. He wanted me to know who he was, in case he didn't make it. His name was Cornelio Martinez. I was to get a message somehow to his mother in Nogales, in the colonia of Solidaridad.

"You'll make it," I said.

"My brother didn't. He died last January, in the cold."

"Doing what?" I asked.

"Smuggling. He couldn't keep up. He had hepatitis."

We staggered through midday and long into the afternoon. I went many places in my mind. I had conversations with many people—my father, Julio, Miguel, my sister Mari Cruz, the priest at the shrine of El Cristo Rey, even with Rico's teacher working at the Laundromat in Los Angeles. She said she could get me a job there and also give me English lessons. She was very beautiful. I told her I would appreciate the English lessons, but I preferred to work outdoors.

Most of my imaginary conversations were with Rico. They weren't really conversations. They were arguments, and he kept defending himself. I told him I should have known better, after what he did to his parents. I told him he was no kind of friend. That ours had never been a friendship of equals.

Once again, the mule train stopped dead. I shook myself back to the present. For the fourth or fifth time, someone had fallen. It was Rico.

He was on his knees, struggling to rise. No one was helping him up. Our eyes met. For a second, I wasn't going to help him. He looked awful. I felt awful. I pulled him to his feet. "Thanks, Turtle," he said.

I didn't know I could produce words, even if I tried. "It's nothing," I managed.

"Victor, I'm not doing so well."

"Same here."

We staggered on, down into a canyon where a seep trickled from a cluster of ferns on a rock ledge. Only one mule at a time could get to the water, and the two of us were going to be the last to drink. Pretty soon it became obvious—the seep ran so slowly, this was going to take hours.

I was light-headed and delirious. I had to get out of the sun, and fast, before I collapsed. Shade was the only thought on my mind, if I was thinking at all. I stumbled off looking for some. The mules were all strung out, tucked in every little piece of shade and waiting their turn at the water. Another hundred yards was an overhanging boulder, if I could reach it.

Around the back side of the boulder I found a sliver of shade. I got down and was wedging myself into it when rattling erupted, fast and angry, unmistakable and close. *Snake!* cried every nerve in my body. I felt the bite in my ankle as I tried to leap away, managing only to hit the top of my head on the boulder.

I must have screamed. Rico came running, along with some others. I never saw the snake, only white pain in my skull. I heard them bashing the devilish thing with rocks. I took off my hat. There was a new rip in the straw. I felt to see if I had a new gash. My fingers came back with only a smear of blood.

"Did it bite you?" Rico was saying.

"Yes," I said, my fear racing out of control. I got down to look at my ankle. The marks of the fangs were plain to see.

"That kid is as good as dead," I heard one of the mules say.

All my life, somehow, I had known this was coming.

23

Escape

THEY LET RICO AND ME get to the water. I drank my fill, and then I drank some more. "Pretty soon his ankle will swell up," Jarra was telling Morales as they watched from the shade of a nearby mesquite. "His whole leg is going to bloat like a carcass. We'll have to leave him behind."

"I give you permission to carry his pack, if that's what you're wondering about," Morales said with a laugh.

Jarra looked at me with hatred, flicked back his forelock and said, "Why not put a bullet in him?"

"Don't listen," Rico whispered. "He's only messing with your mind."

I crawled off to wait for the swelling and the horror to come. "I'll stay behind with you, no matter what," Rico said.

"Don't. He'll put a bullet in you, too."

After an hour, my heart was still racing, my head still pounding, but my ankle and leg were the same as ever. "Calm down," Rico said. "Maybe nothing's going to happen from the snakebite." He fell asleep.

The sun was stuck in the sky. Time dragged. In Arizona, a day in May went on forever. Hours later, the sun was finally sinking. The bump on my head was swollen and I was suffering from the heat, but that was all.

Moonrise wasn't far off. The mules were getting ready to saddle up again, and so was I. They were all talking about me and the rattlesnake, wondering how I could have been so lucky. Paco said there was such a thing as a bite with no poison, and that must be what happened. Jarra gave me a look as if to say he would deal with me later.

I could only think I had been given a miracle. I knew who to thank: the Virgin of Guadalupe, whose image I carried in my pocket, and my mother. She had been lighting candles for me in the village church, same as she used to for my father.

As soon as the moon rose over the mountains, huge and brilliant, we started out. We were going to walk all night again. There was talk about a well. Our direction remained the same: due north, up and down the flanks of the mountains. Late in the night, we came to the bottom of a canyon, and the well. A rugged dirt road ended here. There were tire tracks in the road, which made the mules nervous. Morales went down the road to stand guard as Jarra lowered a bucket. I drank the last of my water.

The bucket struck bottom with a hollow clang. Every mule let out a groan, me included. Jarra went to find Morales. I looked around for Rico, but he wasn't there.

A few minutes later Rico was back. I asked him where he had been. "Call of nature," he whispered. His eyebrows were all knitted together, never a good sign.

"What's wrong?" I whispered back.

"Tell you later."

Morales and Jarra returned. "Saddle up!" Morales ordered.

After that, I couldn't stop worrying. The way Rico was acting, I knew he must have overheard Jarra and Morales, heard them talking about us. But what, what had he heard? What a relief, when dawn finally came, to drop my pack, flop beside it on the ground, and think about food instead.

Each of us was issued two tins of fish and two tortillas. The sardines were salty and packed in mustard. It was difficult to get them past my swollen tongue without water.

"Saddle up!" Morales ordered, all too soon. The sun shot up like a rocket and stuck there, scorchingly high in the sky. I hated the boss as much as I hated Jarra. The head of the centipede, with his light pack, didn't seem to notice that the rest of us had to run to keep up. Somebody was going to drop dead. The sun was practically overhead before Morales, with a grin, finally unslung his rifle. "Find shade," he said. "We'll take a siesta."

The shade was scarce and quickly taken. As usual, Rico and I were going to have to walk the farthest to find any. We exchanged glances as we stumbled along in the heat. "We have to talk," Rico said.

"I haven't forgotten."

We crawled under the branches of a mesquite. "We have to get away," Rico said. "They're going to kill us."

"Did you hear them say that?"

"It's what somebody else heard—Cornelio, from Nogales, the one who fell, and you helped him up. He heard Jarra telling Morales that they couldn't let us go when this was over. That we would talk. That we would identify them."

"Did Cornelio say what Morales said back to Jarra?"

"That Jarra could take care of it. Jarra said he'd be happy to."

"Mother of God! Maybe we should go now, Rico. I think everybody will sleep a while, Morales and Jarra included."

"What about water?"

"Take our chances on finding some?"

"Maybe so. Right here, right now, we have a chance at a head start. We have to hope the siesta is a long one. Do we go down into the valley or up into the mountains?"

"Down below, it's crawling with Border Patrol."

"I was afraid you were going to say that. But these mountains are dry as a bone."

"Miguel said that mountains have water. It's just a matter of finding it."

"Ah, the wise Miguel."

"Rico, shall I strangle you now or later?"

"Later," he said. "I think you're right about going where the Border Patrol aren't."

"These mountains are skinny. We can cross them quickly,

straight across to the other side. We'll hit that paved road from Sasabe up to Tucson."

"We'll get lucky and get a ride."

"We have to hope so."

We got ready. We were going to go light—my pocketknife, a tin of fish in each of our back pockets, our empty water jugs. Rico took a walk back through the mules, to see if any were on their feet. "It's now or never," he said when he got back.

We propped our packs out in the open to make it seem we were close by, then sneaked away. The first patch of solid rock we came to, we started climbing. "They aren't going to follow," I said, "not in this heat."

"Jarra would be crazy enough," Rico said, and I knew he was right.

We kept climbing. Sometimes it was hand over hand. The slope was taking the brunt of the midday sun, and we were drenched with sweat. We climbed out of the foothills and onto the slopes of the higher mountains, above where the giant cactus could grow. "It's much cooler up here," I gasped.

"Your brain is boiling 'mano."

"So is the water in my jug. It's going to burn a hole in the plastic."

"In case you haven't noticed, your jug is empty."

"I'm afraid I will scald my tongue." I took off the cap and pretended to drink. "Now we're both out of water."

"At least no one is following us as we are dying of thirst."

"Thank God for that."

We couldn't keep climbing straight up. The slope was getting even steeper, and was overgrown with cactus and yucca. We angled to the north, climbing more gradually. Eventually we came within sight of a huge canyon down below. We had to find water.

The heat had us feverish, dizzy, stumbling, skinning up our knees and hands. We followed an animal trail around the slope as we approached the canyon. Vultures and caracaras were circling overhead—did we look that bad off?

By Rico's watch, it was four o'clock, four hours since our escape, and still broiling. We angled into the canyon in the direction of some mine tailings and a tumbled-down shack close to the bottom. The slope was steep, strewn with gravel loose as marbles. It was going to take a long time to get down, but we didn't have any choice. There had to be water down there. Without water, a prospector wouldn't have lasted long enough to build a shack. Without water, we weren't going to make it over the mountains.

At the shack, we found nothing but bottles turned purple by the sun, bits of ancient trash, decades of rat droppings. A rusty well casing sticking out of the ground raised our hopes. The pipe was six inches across, wide enough to let us lower one of the bottles inside, if only we could find some cord or wire. But would there be water?

I dropped a small stone down the pipe to find out. It hit with a solid clunk. Rico made a bitter face and swallowed hard. "Maybe farther up the canyon," I said.

The floor of the canyon was smooth as concrete. We rounded a bend and there suddenly was our water, glistening where it dripped out of a seam above the bedrock.

Rico's eyes went to something else, and then I saw, too. To the side and in the full glare of the sun lay the body of a man in uniform, a uniform with a dark green shirt.

"Border Patrol," Rico whispered.

We walked up close. The man was on his back, eyes closed. Flies were buzzing around his round, full face. "His chest is all swollen up," I said.

"That's his body armor, underneath." Rico felt for a pulse at his neck. "He's alive. Heat got him, I guess."

"You think he was after us?"

"Who knows? I'm just wondering if there's more of them."

"Doesn't seem like it," I said, looking over my shoulder. "No shade to drag him into. Maybe water will bring him around."

"What about his gun, that radio, that club, and the can of spray?"

"Hide them?"

"Drop 'em down that pipe we found, where he can't possibly get to them. It's only a couple of minutes back."

"You sure about the radio? Wouldn't he need it to call for help?"

"Are you kidding? Let him call for help? That would be the end of the story for us. If we get him cooled down, and he comes to, he's on his own. Just like we are. Are we going to talk all day?"

We took the patrolman's things, and I hurried away to get rid of them while Rico went to fill our jugs.

At the well casing, I dropped in the gun, the spray, and the club.

The radio in my hand was all that was left. I hesitated. What if water didn't help, and the man still needed to get out? Were we going to let him die? I hurried back, and hid the small radio just before I got to Rico.

The patrolman was up on one elbow, looking around, blinking his eyes as Rico poured water down his broad forehead. His name-plate said TORRES. "Who are you?" was the first thing he said.

"We got abandoned by our pollero," Rico said. "We're trying to climb out."

Suddenly the policeman realized that his gun was missing, his radio and all the rest. "What have you done?"

"Nothing," Rico said.

"Don't lie to me. Where are my things?"

"Down a pipe," I said. "Way, way down."

"Why, why would you do that?" His voice was desperate, strangled.

Rico sort of laughed. "I suppose you were going to let us go?"

"Under the circumstances, yes."

"What circumstances?"

"Look at the back of my head, but don't touch."

We looked. A sharp piece of rock was sticking out of his skull. The hair around it was all matted with blood. Some blood had run down his neck and between his shoulders.

"Ayeee," I said, looking at the thin sharp rock. "What's that doing there?"

"I was in a gun fight. There were rocks and boulders all around us. They sprayed lots of fire off the rocks. This splinter got me in the back of my head."

"Where was this gun battle?" Rico demanded.

"At the mouth of the canyon."

"You want us to pull the rock out?" I asked.

"Don't touch it! You could kill me if you try to pull it out."

"Should we wrap something around it then, so it won't fall out?"

"That might push it in deeper. Just leave it alone."

Torres checked his watch. "I wasn't unconscious long. My partner and I were attacked by drug smugglers."

Rico gave me a nudge. "Let's get out of here, before his partner comes."

"He's dead," the patrolman said with a grimace. "We were outgunned. They've got an assault rifle."

Rico and I exchanged glances. Was it Morales and his mules that Torres had run into at the mouth of this canyon, after their siesta? Was that possible?

"How come you didn't radio for help when you were attacked?" Rico asked.

"No reception. I was trying to climb out of here when I blacked out. There's a trail close by. Higher up, I could get reception. Tell me, please, where you put the radio."

"We already told you," Rico said. "It's way down at the bottom of a pipe."

"God help me," Torres said. "They've cut me off from my vehicle, and they're tracking me right now."

I looked down the canyon, in a panic I would see Jarra, Morales, or both. "How do you know that?"

"Soon as the gunfire let up, I scrambled around to where I could see. It was drug runners, all right. I saw them put their bales on their backs and take off. Two stayed behind. They know I would have a radio on me. They're guessing I haven't gotten through yet, on account of the terrain. One of those two has the assault rifle. I saw them starting after me."

"If they were following you," Rico scoffed, "they would have been here by now."

"They're afraid of ambush, moving slow. I beg you, please, they might be here any minute."

"I've got the radio," I admitted.

24

Speak of the Devil

THE PATROLMAN KNEW EXACTLY where we were—Baboquivari Canyon. Even better, he knew a way out. Nearby was a pack trail that the Indians used to visit Baboquivari Peak, their sacred mountain.

Above us, there would be no more water, Torres said. We drank hastily, filled our jugs, and got going. The trail climbed up and to the south, with many switchbacks, toward a high ridge. The patrolman stopped at every other switchback to catch his breath and look below.

Twenty minutes up, we had to take a longer break and drink some water. "I don't see anybody down there," Rico said. "Maybe you were wrong about them coming after you. Maybe they turned back."

"Hope so." Torres tried his radio, with no luck. "Got to get higher," he said. "Soon as I get through, they'll send a helicopter."

"What will happen to us?" I asked.

"You come with me."

"To be deported?"

"Maybe not. Sometimes, believe it or not, we turn people loose."

"You don't really know what they'll do to us, do you," Rico said, his voice full of anger.

"You're right, I can't say for sure. It's not my decision."

"How can you sleep at night?"

"How do you mean?"

"I mean, how can you work against your own people?"

"Rico," I said. "Stop it."

"Seriously," Rico insisted. "Tell us how you sleep at night."

"I do a job that needs to be done," Torres replied. "I enforce the law. Yes, we do all we can to slow the flood of illegals, but I also save many lives. And we catch some dangerous criminals. Listen, I can't stand here and argue with you. My head hurts bad, and my partner is dead."

The air went out of Rico's anger. "I'm sorry," he said. "I'm sorry about your partner. How did it happen?"

"We were on foot, away from our vehicle. I suspected that the drug smugglers had a trail through the foothills of these mountains. My partner paid for my curiosity with his life—we ran right into them. I have to get word out. These people have to be stopped."

I pointed down the mountain. "Uh-oh."

Far below, two men were winding their way up the switchbacks.

The one in the lead had an assault rifle in one hand, a water bottle in the other. I squinted. He had a green baseball cap worn backward. I even saw a glint of purple. "Jarra," I said.

Torres rose unsteadily to his feet. "Who's he?"

Rico was glaring at me. "One of the coyotes who abandoned us," I said unconvincingly.

"If they've got an automatic weapon like that, you two haven't told me the truth. You weren't simply mojados. You were with them?"

"They're gaining on us," Rico said. "Some other time, we'll tell you our life story."

We climbed as fast as we could, which wasn't very fast. The trail was the steepest yet. There was nothing above us but switchbacks zigzagging into the sky. It was around five-thirty, and the heat hadn't broken. My lungs were burning, my legs felt like rubber. I felt faint, like I might fall over and tumble down the mountain. I wondered how long Torres could hang on. He was ahead of me, and he looked bad. He might black out again any moment. He might drop dead.

I looked over my shoulder. Jarra and the other—one of the mules—were getting closer. Without doubt, they had recognized Rico and me. Jarra had as much reason to hunt us as he did the patrolman. That assault rifle . . . Jarra and the boss must have switched weapons before Morales took off with the rest of the mules.

By the grace of God, we reached the top of the switchbacks. We were on the ridge and Torres had his radio out. I looked over the edge. Jarra and the mule were about five hundred feet below us. "There's no time to get a helicopter," I said.

"And no place for it to land," Rico added. It was true. The face of the ridge was steep and strewn with rubble.

Torres was stumbling along the trail, talking into his radio, telling them to answer. I knelt down and shoved a rock over the edge, twice as big as a soccer ball. Rico and I watched it bounce down the slope, faster and faster, straight at Jarra and the mule. Just before it reached them, it exploded into pieces that went flying in all directions. In the nick of time, they flattened themselves, or else their heads would have been taken off. "You go ahead with the policeman," I said. "I'll stay back and hold them off."

"You sure?"

"I'm sure!" I yelled. "Go!"

I crawled to the edge on my hands and knees, and I peeked over. Jarra was picking himself up, and so was the mule. I started another rock rolling, this one bigger than the first, and watched it bound in huge leaps straight down on them. Unfortunately, it didn't break apart. It bounced twenty feet over their heads, but it had loosened other rocks on its way down, which made them scramble for their lives.

I had them pretty well pinned down. They might think they were out of sight, behind some small boulders, but I could see their legs sticking out. It wasn't going to be easy for them to outflank me. The slope on either side of the trail was too steep for walking. They had to use the switchbacks to come up or to go back down. Either way, they'd be exposed as soon as they stood up.

They knew I had them nailed down. Time dragged. They were waiting me out. They thought I would quit, and keep going up the trail, and then they would catch up.

Twenty minutes might have gone by before they showed themselves. Maybe they thought I had left. I had a beauty of a rock ready for them, practically a boulder. Like a beetle rolling a ball of dung, I had worked it close to the edge. When they made their move, I made mine. I braced and shoved and kicked with both legs, and the rock tipped over the edge.

After bouncing four times, this one exploded, and it did some damage. Not to Jarra, but to the mule. A piece of rock sent him flying. Jarra got off a burst of bullets, shooting wild. He couldn't see me, but I could see him. The mule was dragging one leg as he retreated down the trail.

After that it was just me and Jarra. He kept playing the waiting game, but I wasn't going anywhere, not until I heard that helicopter. The heat was starting to let up, and I had water.

At last Jarra made another move. He must have thought I was gone for good. I wouldn't have rolled another rock if he'd gone back down the trail, but he tried running up it. "Today's butcher is tomorrow's beef," I muttered as I let a good one fly. Jarra had to go flying, too, behind another boulder.

What's taking the helicopter so long? I wondered. Just then I heard it. The sound came from behind me, from over the mountain, not from the Indian reservation. From Tucson, I guessed. I could see the helicopter coming down—it landed out of sight. I took off along the trail fast as I could. I had to hope that down below, Jarra wouldn't have heard the helicopter, would think I still had him pinned down.

When I got there, there was no helicopter and no patrolman. There was only Rico. "What happened?" I panted.

"They got Torres, then they took off."

"Was he okay?"

"I don't know. He was unconscious."

"Had he told them about us?"

"Never got to it. He'd just said into his radio where he was when he blacked out."

"What did you tell the rescue people?"

"They didn't know I was here. I watched from behind a rock."

"Are you crazy, Rico? Jarra's coming! You could have gotten away!"

"I thought about it, but they wouldn't have waited for you. What about Jarra? Are those two still after us?"

"I hit the mule—he turned back. I'm not sure about Jarra. I have a feeling he isn't going to quit."

"Let's go, then!"

The trail kept climbing the spine of the ridge. It was evening, and our shadows long, when the trail finally leveled out on a high bench. Baboquivari Peak was suddenly right there, right in front of us, bigger than all imagination, a tower filling up the sky with soaring faces of solid rock. Placed on top of it, the great statue of El

Cristo Rey would have looked like a tiny toy.

We stopped to breathe deep, and drank the last of our water. The sun was setting as we sat with the mountain at our backs and looked across the reservation and far into Mexico. "We're a long way from home," I said.

At the mention of home, Rico had nothing to say.

"Rico, I still say you should have gotten into that helicopter. No matter what happened, you would have been safe from Jarra."

"Speak of the devil," Rico said, pointing below. "Here he comes."

25

The Broken Ledge

W E COULDN'T LET THAT assault rifle get any closer. Even so, Jarra was gaining on us little by little. All his time in these desert mountains had turned his legs to steel. All we could do was keep climbing the trail, which was aiming toward the ridge at the foot of Baboquivari Peak.

When we finally crested the ridge, we were in a panic. Jarra was minutes behind us, and we had nowhere to go. The trail ended here. Between us and the trees far below, the slopes were open ground, mostly rockslides, with nowhere to hide from Jarra's weapon. "We're done for," Rico panted, eyes casting all around. "What now, Victor?"

Where else, where else could we hide? I tilted my head back and looked up. A short, steep slope separated us from the cliffs, which soared a thousand feet or more to the summit. "Climb?" I wondered aloud. Without waiting for an answer, I dropped my water jug and started up. I climbed fast as I could, reaching for rock holds, the trunk of a stunted tree, tufts of grass, Rico right behind. We were exposed as could be. We had to get our backs out of view before Jarra rounded the corner.

We climbed until we were touching the foot of the cliffs. Half a breath, and we scrambled even higher, up a crack and onto a ledge that sailed out across the lower face of the summit tower. Above us, there was only sheer rock vaulting into the darkening sky. The ledge would keep us out of sight as long as we stayed down.

We listened and we waited—not for long—and then we heard Jarra's steps. He'd reached the end of the trail. He wasn't far below, no more than a hundred feet. No doubt he was scanning the slopes underneath him, surprised he couldn't see us crashing down the other side. By now he was beginning to wonder where else we could be. He might already be looking up. By now he was seeing the fresh marks we had made in the dirt, gravel, and grass where we started our climb. Even if he couldn't see us, he could tell we were up here, and he knew he had us trapped.

It was getting dark. "Villa!" he yelled. "Zapata! What are you doing up there, roosting like chickens for the night?" I could picture him flicking back his donkey tail, aiming the assault rifle in case we showed our heads.

The silence was too much for Jarra to take. He started clucking his head off, and then came the insane laughter of a demon. "It's just a matter of time," he crowed. "You idiots are mine!"

When would he come after us, that was the question. The moon would be bright when it rose, only a few days past full, bright enough for Jarra to climb by. Would he try to surprise us during the night? We had no rocks to throw down on him, but he might not know that. All we had was the pocketknife. "If he climbs up here," Rico said, "go for the rifle before he can use it. Let's try to throw him over the edge."

We were both so exhausted, we didn't know if we'd be able to stay awake. Rico took off his watch and placed it between us. I would sleep first. Every hour, we would trade off.

I was farthest out on the ledge. Rico had the pocketknife clenched in his hand, ready to slash at Jarra if he suddenly appeared. I fell into a deep sleep.

When Rico nudged me awake, it came as a shock to see where I was, and remember how I got there. The moon rose during my first watch. I couldn't see the moon itself, but the far end of the cliffs was already lit. It wouldn't take long for the moonlight to spread across the summit.

I fought my drowsiness. I fought it hard, but still, after a while, I couldn't tell if I was awake or dreaming. Time had passed, and the summit wall was almost completely bathed in moonlight. As I looked out across the face of the peak I saw something moving. I looked again and saw a creature out my dreams, out of my child-hood in Chiapas: a great spotted cat, silently and effortless ghost-ing in our direction.

I blinked and the jaguar was still there, big as life in the silvery light, on a ledge that might connect to ours. I wanted to jab Rico's shoulder, but couldn't take my eyes off the apparition.

The jaguar halted where its ledge narrowed and appeared to end. I held my breath. The jaguar crouched and peered down a steep, nearly vertical break in the cliffs between the higher ledge and ours. To my amazement, the great cat was poised to start down the break. It paused, and looked in my direction. It saw me, or sensed I was there. Just that fast, the jaguar turned around and disappeared.

I slapped myself awake, fully awake. I doubted the jaguar, but not the message, whoever had sent it—maybe my father? One of the jaguar's powers, my father once told me, was invisibility, the ability to move unseen. Maybe Rico and I could cross the peak unseen and escape before Jarra knew we were gone.

Crazy, I thought, but maybe it was possible. I nudged Rico, and he woke with a start.

He grabbed his watch. "It isn't my time yet. You falling asleep?"

"I'm wide awake, 'mano."

I told him about my tigre. He looked across the ledge, completely lit now. I pointed out the spot two-thirds of the way across where our ledge met the steep connection to the upper ledge. I told him that the jaguar had intended to use that break to reach our ledge and cross the peak. "We can do the same from this end," I said.

"I'm not as big on signs and miracles as you are," Rico said, "but Jarra's going to slaughter us in the morning. I'm willing to take the chance. Not to go first, though. I'll be right behind, as long as it looks good to you. You would never try to do anything too crazy."

"Okay," I said. "I'm pretty sure this is what we have to do." I started out. At first it was easy, but then the footing got tricky. The ledge was brightly lit, but there were loose rocks to step over and the fall was sickeningly deep—a hundred, two hundred feet. As the corner of my eye barely took it in, my vision swam and I went lightheaded with the sensation of falling. I pictured my body crumpled on the rocks below.

Don't do that, I told myself. Calm down. Believe you have four legs, the power and the balance of the jaguar. I took a deep breath.

We were halfway across. Our ledge had narrowed from six feet to two. The quiet footfalls of Rico followed close behind. So much for being the cautious one, I thought.

Here came the hardest part. The ledge was down to a foot wide, and then nothing. I had reached the break between ledges, where my route angled up fifteen feet or more. If it couldn't be done, I was turning right around.

My heart began to race. I started to go dizzy again. My stomach was cramping, I went all weak in my legs. I felt like I was going to peel off the cliff and fall any second. The worst part was, I thought I saw handholds and footholds above me in the moonlight.

All I could reach for now was my family. I saw my mother's face. I heard her voice: *"Think of us, and it will help. Always know, you are never alone."*

With that, I knew I was going to go through with it. I felt the strength flowing back into my mind and my legs. I reached for my first handhold. For Chuy, I thought. Climb like a jaguar, for Chuy and the girls, for my mother. I reached, and my legs followed.

Just like a train ladder, I thought. Up I went. Reach and pull and lift. Reach and pull and lift. No slowing, no stopping, no thinking. I was almost there. My hands found the upper ledge and I was able to climb onto it. It was okay up there, plenty wide. This ledge would take us the rest of the way across. I held tight, my back against the cliff, hoping Rico was right behind.

I waited. This was taking too long. "I'm having some trouble getting started," I heard him call.

"Take your time," I said.

"I can't believe what you just did. I'm afraid to take the first step, and after that, it's practically straight up."

"I can't help you from here."

"I know. You've already helped me plenty, Turtle."

Suddenly I liked the name. "Come on up here, 'mano. Everything is good. Pretend you're climbing a ladder."

"All is forgiven? Best friends again?"

"Best friends."

"Brothers? Like it used to be?"

"Brothers. Yesterday, you risked your life to stay with me. Right now, I'm not going anywhere without you."

"If it was daytime, maybe. I just don't think I can do it."

"Think about it, Rico. If I just did it, you can do it easier. Your legs are longer, and you're really strong. Think about a reason you have to make it."

"Like, I'll be dead if I don't?" he joked weakly.

"I mean the biggest reason you have to live."

An awful silence followed, then at last, "Here I come."

I could hear him scratching his way up, but then he stopped. Just stopped, gasping for breath. "You're close," I called. "Almost here."

Finally he was moving again. As he came over the top, I reached for his hand and pulled him onto the ledge. His knees were shaking. "Thank God," he said. He was utterly spent.

A good rest, and then we crossed the rest of the ledge. Overjoyed to be off the peak, we plunged into the forest with abandon. On the eastern side, the mountain was thickly wooded with pines, oaks, and junipers. As we started down a steep canyon, we had to go slow. I dislodged a rock, and three startled deer went bounding away.

We stayed in the canyon bottom except to walk around the dry waterfalls. At dawn we came across a wet spot on the sand with hundreds of small golden butterflies all bunched together. We got close, and they fluttered into the air, dissolving and disappearing like particles of a dream.

Farther down, thousands of feet down, we came out of the trees. The slopes were covered with mesquite scrub, yucca, and cactus. We came across a spring, where a metal pipe rammed into a mossy patch on the mountainside led to a holding tank filled to overflowing. A short pipe sticking out from the top of the tank spilled a steady flow of cold, clear water onto the ground.

We drank and drank, then ate our tins of fish. We laughed about Jarra, how confused he must be trying to figure out what happened. Around the bend we came to a corral, which made us wary.

The sight of a small ranch house sent us scurrying like rats. We skirted it carefully, seeing no vehicles or other signs of life.

A dirt road led away from the ranch house toward the valley below. We decided to make use of it, but to be ready to run into the scrub at the first sound of a motor. We walked a couple of miles east. The highway running north to Tucson had to be within reach. Eventually we heard the sound of a vehicle in low gear. We jumped aside and hid. From our hiding place we could see it coming up the road, in and out of the gullies. It was the shape of a perrera but didn't have the colors. It was dark red. "Here comes our ride," Rico said.

"Wait a minute. See his face?"

"He has a beard. So what?"

"You know what I mean. That's a gabacho."

"So?" Rico said. "From what I hear, some even scatter water in the desert, to keep people from dying of thirst."

"Miguel never said if they could be trusted. I guess it's a risk we'll have to take. Just be ready to run, okay?"

Right in the middle of the road, that's where we stood. We held our hands up to signal for help.

The driver stopped. The gabacho's beard was partly blond, partly red. Rico tried to talk to him in English, but couldn't find the words.

"I speak some Spanish," the man said. He was neither young nor old. His face was freshly sunburned.

"Is that your ranch up there?" Rico asked.

The driver was looking us up and down. "No, not mine."

"We need some help," I said.

"It looks like you've come a long way. Lost your backpacks? Had some trouble?"

"Lots. We need a ride. Can you help us?"

"I wish I could . . . I have work to do. I study animals, up ahead here."

"But can't you do your work later? Help us now?" Rico asked.

"Tell you what," he said. "This evening I'll be driving back out. If you're still on this road, maybe I can do something for you."

We thanked him. He drove on, and we kept walking out. "He was thinking about it," I said.

Rico heaved a shrug. "Who knows what he was really thinking. Looked to me like he was afraid of getting in trouble if he helped us."

Ten minutes down the road, we heard a vehicle *behind* us, and we ran like quail. It turned out to be the same red truck, same gabacho. We came cautiously into the open. His window went down. "I'll take you as far as Tucson," the man said. "No farther."

This seemed too good to be true. Why had he come back for us? I wondered.

"My brother lives there," Rico said. "In Tucson. That would be perfect. Should both of us get in the back?"

"Not both. That would draw attention."

I got in the front. "Buckle your seatbelt," the gabacho told me.

"My name's Dave Hansen," he said, starting down the road. "What are yours?"

I hesitated. "How come you turned around and came back?"

"You guys look pretty ragged. In the last three days, twelve people have died in the desert. My work can wait."

"Rico Rivera's my name," Rico called from the back. "That's my good friend in the front seat, Victor Flores. He's returning to his cautious ways. You can call him Turtle."

"Do we need to duck down whenever there's a car?" I asked.

The driver laughed. "Relax," he said. "Unless we run into a roadblock for all cars, the Border Patrol isn't going to stop us."

When we got to the pavement, Hansen turned north. Tucson, I remembered from the map, was north and east. I was tense as could be. I kept looking ahead in fear I would see cars stopping for a roadblock, like the one past Guadalajara where the customs police made me get off the bus. Half an hour later we reached the intersection with the highway from the west, the one that crosses through the reservation, the one our mule train must have been headed for.

I shivered to see three Border Patrol vehicles parked at the highway junction, two at the café and one at the gas pump. We took a right, toward Tucson. A little farther on we passed a Migra machine on the side of the road. Hansen called it a cyclops. It was a hoist with a policeman sitting in a box high in the air, watching the brush through huge binoculars. "The Border Patrol catches a lot of people as they're nearing the highway," Hansen said. "Relax, Victor."

"I'll try," I said. "What kind of animals do you study?"

"Not turtles," he said. "I study the tigre."

"You mean puma?"

"No, not the mountain lion. I'm talking about a cat that's even bigger, and covered with beautiful spots—the Mexican tigre. Its English name is jaguar."

"I thought you had to go far down in Mexico to find them, close to Guatemala. . . ."

The man shook his head and smiled. "To find very many, that's true. They used to live in southern Arizona a long time ago, and now a few are moving north again, across the high desert from the Sierra Madre. I check on my 'scratchers'—little fur catchers I tack to the trees—and I check my cameras. A couple months ago I got a picture of a jaguar at the head of the canyon you came down. That was at night, with a trip wire. What I wouldn't give to see that magnificent animal in person."

"I did," I said. "Last night."

Hansen turned to stare straight at me. "You're telling me you saw a jaguar in these mountains? Are you sure?"

"I saw one once before, and I've also seen a puma. I know the difference."

"Where did you see a jaguar before? In a zoo?"

"In the wild. In Chiapas, close to Guatemala."

Hansen reached over and touched my arm. "Maybe your luck will rub off on me. Where exactly did you see the one last night?"

"It was crossing the ledge across the peak."

Hansen pounded his steering wheel. "Fantastic! I can watch for that! Funny thing . . . every once in a while, mountain climbers cross there before they break out their ropes and go for the summit. They call it the Lion's Ledge. From now on, at least in my book, it's the Jaguar's Ledge."

26

T
HE JAGUAR MAN RECOGNIZED the name of the street that Rico's brother lived on. He used to live nearby. There were many stoplights to wait for, shopping centers to pass by, beautiful palm trees. Rico had come a long, long way to be this silent so close to his destination. The neighborhood Hansen turned into was filled with houses beyond the wildest dreams of anyone from Los Árboles. I myself was daring to dream that I would be able to work alongside Rico cleaning the swimming pools. If not, his brother might let me clean the cars that he bought and sold.

Hansen braked across the street from the number we were looking for, 321. He let us out. He said he would go and get gas, then come back to see how things turned out.

We stood on the sidewalk across the street. I felt like hiding as cars went by. Some of the drivers were talking on cell phones. All it would take was for one of them to call the Border Patrol.

"Reynaldo is married, I know that much," Rico said. "I know he has kids, but I don't know how many or anything about them."

"What are you getting at?"

"I'm thinking Reynaldo must be away at work. I don't see a truck for his swimming pool business."

"There's a car. Probably his wife is home. Go find out."

"It all comes down to this," Rico said. "All my hopes and dreams, and I feel sick."

"Go, 'mano! I'll be waiting right here."

I sat on the curb. Rico dragged himself across the street and up to the front door. He pressed a button. A woman with a curly dog in her arms came to the door. They talked. Something wasn't right. She was shaking her head. She pointed to the next house, then closed the door.

Rico called me over. "It's this house over here. She wouldn't explain—I must have got the number wrong. I want you to come with me."

"Okay," I said.

The man who answered the door was mostly bald and very well fed. "I'm Rico," Rico said. The man stared at him. "Reynaldo, it's me, your youngest brother, all the way from Los Árboles."

"I'm not Reynaldo," the man said, as a boy of nine or ten came to the door and stared. The boy was drinking a can of soda.

It took a few seconds to unravel the confusion. Rico had the address right in the first place. Reynaldo lived next door, or used to. The neighbor explained that Reynaldo and his family had left in the middle of the night, about three weeks ago.

"Why?" Rico asked.

"He would have been arrested. His family would have been deported."

"Arrested for what?"

"Stealing cars!" the boy blurted out.

"SUVs, vans, and pickups," the neighbor said. "Every week or so, there'd be a new one in front of his house. We believed him when he said he was buying and selling them. He always said it was a way to make some extra money."

"Omar's in jail!" the boy interrupted.

"Who's Omar?" asked Rico.

"One of Reynaldo's sons," the man answered. "Omar was always getting into trouble."

"Why was Omar arrested?"

The neighbor grimaced, and said, "The police have connected him to something really awful."

"What is it?"

"Just a couple of hours before Reynaldo took off, there had been a shooting during a high-speed chase on the freeway. One coyote group got crazy-mad at another, for taking their mojados."

"Four people got killed," the boy exclaimed. "The two coyotes in front and two of the mojados under the camper shell."

"That's enough, Juan," his father said. "Go back to your PlayStation."

"You think Reynaldo's son was really involved?" Rico asked.

"He was in the van that did the shooting. The police think that Reynaldo and his son were stealing vehicles to be used in smuggling wets across the border."

The neighbor looked at his watch. "That's all I know." He reached for the doorknob.

I wondered if Rico was thinking what I was thinking. If we had arrived here earlier and started working for Reynaldo, we might have been criminals and not even known it.

"Can you help us out?" Rico pleaded. "We have nowhere to go. We were hoping to find work."

"Sorry," the man said, and then his face hardened. "I can't get myself or my family involved in this." He closed the door on us.

As we walked across the street, Rico's eyes weren't even focusing. "I had no idea," he said.

"Maybe your father was right," I said.

"What are you talking about?"

"Your father told me Reynaldo wasn't honest. Maybe he knew something."

"When? When did my father tell you that?"

"Right after you left. When I had to tell them you'd gone north."

"Why didn't you tell me about this before?"

"When we met in Nogales, I started to tell you about that night. You cut me off. You didn't want to hear anything about your parents."

Rico kicked the curb. "Okay, let's forget about that. The question is, what do I do now? What do we do now?"

"We find work," I said. "What else?"

"Didn't that gabacho who gave us a ride say he'd come back? What's taking him so long?" Rico's face flushed with anger. "I bet he's long gone."

199

"Well, he said he would take us to Tucson and he did."

"He lied, Victor. He said he was going to come back after he got gas, and he didn't. Now what do we do?"

"Figure out how to get to La Perra Flaca, where there's work in the onions and the chilies. Miguel might be there."

"Ah, the great Miguel."

"I know you're disappointed, Rico."

"*Disappointed* isn't a strong enough word."

Just then, a red vehicle rounded the corner, the bearded man at the wheel. The window came down. "I got something to eat," Hansen said. "I hope you like burgers and fries and Cokes."

We ate at a small park nearby, on a table under a cottonwood tree. Rico explained about his brother leaving in the middle of the night, but nothing about why. Hansen asked what we were going to do next. I told him about La Perra Flaca and Miguel, how we needed another ride.

The jaguar man was giving it some thought. "Hitchhiking, you'd have no chance."

"Do you have any ideas?" I asked hopefully.

"Only one. Let's go for another drive."

"Many thanks," Rico and I both said at once.

"But no farther. Not to Chicago."

We drove east on the interstate with me expecting a Border Patrol roadblock any minute. An hour and fifteen minutes is a long time to hold your breath. By the grace of God, Hansen got off the freeway at Willcox without being stopped. His map showed a dead-end road going north but no marked towns.

Our gabacho friend went to ask directions at the KFC. I thought of my little brother. When my family would go to Silao, Chuy would beg to eat there, but we couldn't afford it. Chuy always called it "The Little Old Man."

Hansen came back chuckling. "I should have guessed. The Skinny Dog is just a nickname—Mexican humor. La Perra Flaca has another name—Winchester Heights. It's fifteen or twenty miles up a gravel road, but it's not marked. If we leave Cochise County, we've gone too far."

We started into the desert on the gravel road. Now it was my turn to have my hopes as high as the sky. All my thoughts were on my lone wolf. "Wait for me there," Miguel had said. "I'll be along."

Was he waiting for me? I had a powerful feeling that he was. If they deported him as quickly as before, he would be there by now.

"This has to be it," Hansen said. We had just topped a rise. Ahead lay many dozens of trailers and small houses scattered across the desert.

The street into La Perra Flaca was as rough as any road I'd seen along the border. The fourth trailer looked like it must be a store. It had a Coke machine. Dave Hansen came to a stop in front of it. We knew better than to ask him to wait. He had a long way to go to get back to Baboquivari Peak. We thanked him as we were getting out. "It's nothing," he said.

I told him that my family would always be in his debt.

"Good luck to you both."

"And to you," I said. "I hope you see the jaguar."

He drove away with a smile on his face.

Rico was wrinkling his nose at the smell of raw sewage. I remembered a remark of Miguel's and was confident we'd found the right place. We would soon find out our fate. "La Perra Flaca?" I asked a man coming out the trailer door with a bag of potato chips.

"Yes," he said.

The woman behind the counter knew Miguel, but from the year before. "If he had arrived," she said, "I would have recognized him." She reached for her burning cigarette and pulled deeply on the smoke, her face all bones and hollows. She had sorrowful eyes.

My disappointment was deep. So was Rico's—he looked sick. For all his comments, he had been counting on Miguel, too. "The Border Patrol must have put him in jail," I said.

"Maybe not," said the woman. "From what I hear, everyone is being bused back to the border. So many are coming across, there's no room in the jails."

"I hope you are right, but if so, he would have come here."

"I'm sorry. Bad luck comes in many shapes and sizes. What else can I do for you boys?"

"Is there work here?"

"Not enough," the sad lady said. "The onions are about gone, and the early work on the chilies is mostly done. Many of the workers are leaving."

"Where are the fields? I didn't see any."

"Most of them are an hour away."

"How long would we have to wait until the work picks up?"

She reached for her cigarette. "July. Until the chilies begin to ripen."

27

A Long Ride in the Dark

WE SAT IN THE SHADE of the trailer and licked our wounds. We were as bad off as we looked, all covered with scratches and festering cactus needles. "Welcome to El Norte," Rico said with heavy sarcasm.

"At least we made it this far."

"Look around—we're nowhere."

"Nobody said it was going to be easy."

Rico looked at me sourly, but then he calmed down. We tried to think it through about Miguel.

"I still think they must have put him in jail," I said. "If they let him out recently, he's on his way."

"Who knows what happened? When you come north, nothing can ever be known. What became of Fortino and the three others I started out with from home? Were they robbed, were they tortured? Are they still in jail? Are they in the States? Did they go home?"

"I know what you mean. Maybe we'll never know. I keep wondering about Julio, my friend I told you about, with the inner tube. I wonder if he really made it. Or if he might still be trying to get across."

"What about Torres, the Migra patrolman? Did he die in that helicopter, and what about Jarra and Morales? Did they get caught? Did they get away?"

"I think about those things, too. I think about how my family is doing. I don't have any idea."

"Up here you don't know anything. It stinks. La Perra Flaca stinks, the whole thing stinks."

"It looks like it's you and me, 'mano, whatever happens."

"You're right about that. At least we have each other."

We went back into the store and asked some more questions. The sad woman, whose name was Señora Perez, said that a labor contractor was coming soon, possibly that evening, to pick up workers for the asparagus harvest in the state of Washington. "What is asparagus?" I asked.

"If I had a can I would show you. I've never eaten any myself. It's a green thing that comes out of the ground like a spear, without any leaves or anything."

"Washington sounds good," I said, "but Miguel told me to wait here."

"That would have made sense a month ago. Miguel knows there's no work now. If he shows up, I'll tell him where you have gone."

The state of Washington turned out to be a long, long way. The journey took two days and the night in between. We traveled in darkness, almost thirty hiding in the back of a big rental truck. It was hot in there, but bearable. We heard the story about some wets who fried to death in the trunk of a car.

Stopping for food along the way was too risky. Rico and I had no food. The mojados gave us this and that from their backpacks. The bathroom stops were few—side roads the driver knew about, with trees to run behind. In Idaho, I caught a glimpse of endless fields of green. Potatoes, the mojados said. "Do they grow corn here?" I asked. "Yes," came the answer, "but machines do all the work."

At the end of the journey we got out in Dayton, a small town in the eastern part of Washington. A couple hours farther north, we heard, and we would have been in Canada. Five hours west, we would have seen the ocean.

The countryside was beautiful to my eyes: great rolling hills blanketed with waving wheat, and above them, mountains they called the Blues, all covered with trees. On the flat ground between Dayton and Waitsburg, the next town, there was much asparagus to be harvested.

The work was hard, and it took skill. You move along the row, reaching down to cut the spears just below the ground with a long-handled knife. Cut too deep, and you damage the plant. If they aren't long enough, you leave them for the next day. You have to be fast, because you get paid for how much you pick. We were going to be able to work ten hours a day, six days a week.

Right from the start, I was making around sixty dollars a day, the same amount Julio and Miguel had talked about. Sixty dollars a day! Rico was making around forty. Enrique, the labor boss, gave us $50 each to get by on until the first payday, which couldn't arrive too soon.

Enrique had a distinguished silver mustache and a limp. I wondered if Rico saw the resemblance to his father. I didn't ask. Enrique told us who to see about fake green cards and Social Security cards. "They'll let you pay later," he said. "You'll get by with those. Nobody wants to check up. Just don't think they will fool anyone at the border."

Rico and I lived in a dormitory close to the cannery. It was clean and had hot showers. My first time, I turned on the cold and stood under it, which gave Rico a good laugh. Then I scalded myself, and finally I got the idea.

There were two stores in town with used clothes that people had given away. The clothes cost us so little, they were practically free. The food at the grocery store was expensive, but we never went hungry. Our little notebook, where we kept track of our earnings, told us we were making a lot of money.

The asparagus was going to last until the middle of June. Then it would be time to harvest the cherries somewhere else in Washington. After the cherries, we heard there might be a problem finding work for a few weeks. But then the plums would be ripening. Next would come the peaches. Apples would last into October. I found out how lucky we had been to find work in the asparagus. Little would be grown here next year. The cannery was going to close because Americans were buying their canned asparagus from Peru.

I was learning all this and more from a friend I had made, Pablo Ortega, who had seven kids back in Morelos. Pablo told me about his migrations and those of most of the mojados I was working with. By the middle of October, they would be leaving for Florida, Arizona, or California to pick oranges, lemons, or grapefruit.

For the winter, Pablo himself was going to go someplace near San Francisco, to wait in the parking lot of a store called the Home Depot. He would work each day for whatever person drove up and hired him. He might plant trees, build fences, help people move their things from an old house to a new house—whatever they wanted. He said Rico and I could come along. If you were lucky you could make some good money, but winter wasn't really the best time. Some days there were forty men in the parking lot trying to get work and only a few people coming to hire laborers.

I told Pablo I would be thinking about it, but I was pretty sure I would rather work in the orchards.

Pablo told me to be careful with the good asparagus money. There would be times when work was scarce and times with no work at all. There would be times I would be paid little and charged a lot to sleep elbow to elbow with other mojados on the floors of trailers.

As Rico worked in the asparagus he didn't say much, to me or to anybody. He had no interest in getting to know the other men. They often sang as they worked, and made jokes, but Rico never broke a smile. I tried to encourage him, told him that this was everything we had struggled for. I got nowhere. Whatever he was going through, he didn't want to talk about it. I knew he felt terrible, but I couldn't tell what he was thinking.

The last day of May was payday. By then we'd worked eleven days, and had made an astounding amount of money. I was going to be able to send two hundred and fifty dollars home. Two hundred and fifty dollars!

The very thought of my mother holding that money order in her hand put me on a mountaintop of happiness. The next time, I would be able to send a lot more.

Gone was the fear of my family having to leave home, the fear of my mother ever having to beg on the street. No more hunger in our house, never again if I could help it. That's right, Chuy, have another helping. New clothes for everyone, and my sisters could start thinking about school!

In order to cash our paychecks, Rico and I walked from the dormitory to the main street. Pablo came along to show us how to wire the money.

At the IGA—the big grocery store—the lady behind the office counter spoke Spanish. First she gave me cash for my paycheck. Pablo showed me how to fill out the paper. It had to be done very carefully, with my mother's three names as required. From memory, I printed the exact address of the Western Union in Silao where she was expecting it. I printed my own name carefully, then the amount I was sending, $250.

I handed the paper back to the lady, along with the cash. She asked if my mother had an ID to present in Silao. I said that she did. The lady filled out the paper for me to keep, and showed me the line with a special number in case there was any problem. "Ten dollars more for the transaction," she said. "Fifteen if you want it to arrive today. Otherwise it will arrive tomorrow."

"Tomorrow is good," I told her. "I don't know when exactly my mother will come for it."

I walked away from the counter. My heart was soaring. This had to be the greatest feeling in the world.

There's a part of the store where roasting chickens go around and around on spits, like on the carts in Mexico. I bought one for Rico and me to share by the river, along with some other things. Pablo was meeting some friends at the pool hall.

On the sidewalk outside the store, I waited for Rico. I was still overjoyed at the thought of my mother at the Western Union—the moment she first heard that a money order had arrived, and then when she saw the amount. She would ask them to turn the dollars into pesos. They would hand her around 2,700 pesos.

Two thousand, seven hundred pesos! My mother's tears would flow on that money, not only for the amount, but also to know, after eleven long weeks, I had made it safely across the wire. If only I could see the faces of my sisters and my little brother when she brought home the money and the news.

28

R ICO AND I WALKED along the embankment above the river. It was a small stream with clear, cold water, trout darting here and there. After all this time and all we went through together, I thought, I still don't understand my friend. Why is he so unhappy?

It was a beautiful evening in the park in Dayton, Washington. Everything was green as could be. A breeze was blowing through the cottonwood trees. The long days of searing heat in the desert were almost hard to imagine. We could hear the cheerful shouts of kids playing in the nearby swimming pool. Whatever was knitting Rico's eyebrows together was a mystery to me.

I set out our comida on the table: chicken, small plastic tubs of beans, noodles, and chili peppers, a large Coke for me and a large Dr. Pepper for him. "I'm looking forward to working in the orchards," I said. "They say you get to eat the ones that drop. Eat till you explode."

"I'm not so sure about the orchards," Rico replied.

I had a bad feeling about what this might mean. At least he seemed willing to talk. "What else would we do, 'mano?"

"I'm thinking about doing something completely different," he said.

"Like what? We're making good money!"

"I'm not very good at field work, just like you predicted when I first told you I was going north."

"I never said you wouldn't be good. I just said you wouldn't *like* it."

"I've been thinking about school," Rico said.

"School? How? Even if they let you go to school here, how would you support yourself?"

"Not here, Victor. I'm talking about school back in Silao. I'm thinking about going back to live with my sister."

I was stunned. "After all we've been through, with good money to be made here? Did I miss something? Did you fall off that mountain ledge and land on your head?"

Finally, I'd gotten him to laugh. "Seriously," he said. "I've been thinking about going home."

"Give it a few months, 'mano. You'll get used to the work. The money will add up. Rico, I can't believe you would give up your dreams. You can buy things—a new CD player, lots of CDs. You could even get a car eventually. If you stay up here long enough, they might even change the laws so you can become a citizen. Isn't that what you wanted?"

"Or we could get deported tomorrow, next week, next month . . ."

"Let's hope we don't. But even if we did, we would come back."

"Crossing the border again, through the danger and the stupidity, around and around and around."

"As many times as it takes, remember?"

"It's different for you, Victor."

"Nothing's different."

Rico looked me in the eye. "*Everything's* different. You have a family to send your money back to. A reason to keep you going. But me, why am I here?"

"One day you'll have your own family."

"That's not what I'm talking about."

"What *are* you talking about, then?"

"On the mountain . . . when we were crossing that ledge—that was crazy, you know."

"I know. We were desperate."

"I was so sure I was going to fall. You told me to think about the reason I needed to live, and that would give me the strength. Well, it worked."

"What was it?"

"I hate to admit it. The reason was my parents."

"Your parents? Really? I thought you had put them out of your mind."

"I know, that's what I told you. It never really worked. I was always thinking about them, how they were doing and what I had done."

"So . . . this isn't just about going back to school."

"It's everything. I want to knock on my parents' door. I want to see their faces."

"They would be overjoyed."

"I'm pretty sure you're right."

"I know I'm right."

"I'm worried about my mother, too. You said she'd been to the clinic. I keep—"

A police car was driving by the park. It slowed when the policeman spotted us. He went even slower, taking a long look. We practically stopped breathing. He drove on by.

"If you do this," I said, my heart still racing, "if you go home, I will miss you a lot."

"You'll find friends, Turtle, people to crawl with."

"I know, but I can tell already, people will come and go. It would never be like you and me."

"This is the hardest part for me, leaving you here alone. I believe you when you say you're going to miss me, even if you shouldn't. I know it's going to be really lonely for you up here in El Norte. Back in Silao, I'll think about you all the time, what you've seen and how you're getting along. The good part is that you can send letters to your family—send them to me in Silao, and I will take them to your mother myself."

"I still can't believe this."

"Who knows, maybe someday I'll get back. But it won't be very soon, not for a long time. Not while my parents are alive. I used to think it was unfair that my parents had chosen me to be the one to take care of them in their old age. Now, I choose it."

*

Two days later, on the second of June, we waited at the bus stop on Dayton's main street. We talked about how Rico would be able to tell my mother in person that the money order was waiting for her in Silao, if she hadn't picked it up already. I said I could picture the feast his mother would make to welcome him home. The bus came into view and words got hard to come by. Our arms reached out and we embraced. Our tears ran together. I whispered how proud I was of him. We said good-bye. Rico boarded the bus. "Travel well," I told him.

"You too, 'mano," he said, and then he was gone.

Rico's journey home was going to be straight as an arrow. My journey in search of work would take me in all directions across the States, always looking over my shoulder. All I knew was, I had to survive here, so that my family could survive at home. It might be many long years before I saw them again.

I watched Rico's bus get smaller and smaller. It wasn't the first time I had seen my best friend go out of my life, but it might be the last.

The bus wound its way through the fields and vanished down the river. I wondered if Rico was thinking what I was thinking, that we had finally become true brothers. I was happy, but in a sad sort of way. I remembered one of my father's sayings, one that had always puzzled me: "Sorrow also sings, when it runs too deep to cry." Now I understood.

Author's Note

I'd been visiting Arizona's borderlands for several decades, and contemplating a border story for nearly as long. In the wake of the terrorist attacks of September 11, 2001, the majority of illegal crossings along the U.S./Mexican border were deflected from populated areas to the most remote deserts and mountains of Arizona, with more and more people dying every year. I was moved to learn all I could, and to write a story that would put a human face on the complex and controversial subject of illegal immigration.

In the fall of 2003, I scouted border locations where the latter part of my story might be set. I would like to thank Ann Rasor, the Superintendent of Tumacácori National Historical Park, and her daughter Rae, for hiking with me to Baboquivari Peak. I saw the jaguar "scratchers" and gazed up at the Lion's Ledge, and I knew that somehow both would figure in my story.

I would also like to thank Dan Wirth, Senior Special Agent and Border Coordinator, U.S. Department of the Interior, for the generous and extensive interview he gave me in Tucson on law enforcement issues along the Arizona/Mexican border.

I had traveled to Mexico's state of Guanajuato, and that helped somewhat in choosing a starting point for my protagonist. Victor's fictional village of Los Árboles owes a large debt to the experiences of my niece, Annie Morrissey, who worked as a volunteer in Mexico for a summer through Amigos de las Américas. Annie lived with a family in a village off a back road between the cities of Guanajuato and Silao. The village lies below the mountaintop statue of El Cristo Rey, at the geographical center of Mexico. I drew heavily on my niece's anecdotes and observations as well as her affection for her Mexican family. Thank you, Annie.

As I researched the novel, I drew on countless newspaper stories, magazine and Internet articles, and television documentaries. Of the many books I read, the following are the ones I found most helpful: *Coyotes*, by Ted Conover (Vintage Books, 1987); *The Devil's Highway*, by Luis Alberto Urrea (Little, Brown, 2004); *Diary of an Undocumented Immigrant*, by Ramón "Tianguis" Pérez (Arte Público Press, University of Houston, 1991); *Tunnel Kids*, by Lawrence J. Taylor and Maeve Hickey (University of Arizona Press, 2001); *Folk Wisdom of Mexico*, by Jeff M. Sellers (Chronicle Books, 1994); and *Southern Arizona Nature Almanac*, by Roseann Beggy Hanson and Jonathan Hanson (University of Arizona Press, 1996).

Given rapidly changing conditions, *Crossing the Wire* needed to be grounded in a specific year. I chose 2004, when I did most of the writing.

Durango, Colorado
April 2005